NEIGHBORS LIKE THAT

CARINA TAYLOR

ISBN: 9781692529697

Editor: Jenn Lockwood
Cover designer: Cover Ever After

❀ Created with Vellum

Chapter One

KYLIE

"How ridiculous."

I watched as my new neighbor glanced around, checking for witnesses, before he stuffed two large garbage bags into my garbage can. He leaned on the lid with all of his weight, shoving it closed before jogging back across the street to his house. It was as if he hadn't just used up valuable space in my tiny garbage can.

A garbage can that size was built to accommodate one person—possibly half a person—not a neighbor who brings his jumbo-sized garbage bags from across the street.

I continued glaring at his house, willing it to burst into flames.

Two weeks ago, I saw the moving truck across the street. The home had been recently finished and had only been for sale for a week before someone took down the "For Sale" sign. Wanting to welcome the new neighbors, I baked cookies to take to them. I made chocolate chip cookies from scratch, and they were delicious.

As I knocked on their door, I'd expected a middle-aged couple or maybe a young family with kids—the regular residents you'd expect to find in the suburbs with a picky HOA president. I was the only person under thirty who lived in this neighborhood. An oddity, for sure.

I couldn't have been more surprised when a young, handsome man opened the door. He was the type of handsome that makes you forget your name. In fact, I didn't remember why I was standing on his doorstep.

Dark-blond hair, strong jaw, green eyes, and white teeth that weren't perfectly straight, giving him a carefree air. He was tan, but it was the I-spend-a-lot-of-time-outdoors tan, not the I-spend-a-lot-of-time-with-my-tanning-lotion tan. He was nearly six feet tall and in fantastic shape. I checked his left hand but didn't see a ring.

I had been adequately appreciative of the new scenery until he snapped in my face.

His first words were, and I quote, "I'm not looking for a girlfriend." I informed him—politely, of course—that I wasn't either and that he could go jump in a lake.

Since then, our interaction has been minimal. Oh, and I kept the cookies. They were extra delicious after that.

We haven't said a word to each other since then. A glare here and there and a few angry honks when we pull out of our driveways at the same time have been the only other interactions we've had.

Until this morning, when I'd witnessed the little sneak stuffing his garbage bags into my trash can.

Come to think of it, last week my can had been fuller than usual. Today, most likely, wasn't a first-time offense.

I couldn't let this continue. I *wouldn't* let this continue.

Not when he had so rudely thought I showed up on his doorstep to hit on him. Never mind that he was gorgeous. No amount of handsome could make up for that sense of entitlement.

I released the blinds that I was peeking through.

If I didn't hurry, I would be late for work. I had more important things to do than spy on my annoying neighbor using my trash can.

Last year, I landed my job at a marketing firm as a lead marketer and have loved every minute of it. I've kept my team running smoothly, and I've built a good rapport with my boss. I didn't want to do anything to mess that up. I was young compared to other lead marketers, but my boss had seen my youth as an advantage. She wanted someone who would make a lifelong career at SV Marketing, and I was only too happy to oblige her.

Even though I was relatively new to the job, I bought this house after my first six months in town. It was something I planned on doing ever since I'd graduated college. I'd always wanted a cute house in the suburbs where I could one day raise my family.

That's not what every girl dreams about—believe me, I knew. My old roommate teased me about how basic I was and that I was "settling" because I wanted to get married and have a family. It didn't matter that she was constantly telling me to pursue my dreams. She only wanted me to pursue dreams that she approved of. She continually told me I needed to find a better dream. Except, I knew exactly what I wanted in life, and her "advice" was simply annoying. I began the process of getting approved for a home loan after one of her tirades.

Mimi, my grandma on my dad's side, helped me buy the house by loaning me a large amount for a down payment. She told me, "Every woman needs a place of her own and a little nest egg." She'd also given me a pile of advice on not rushing marriage, which was funny coming from someone who had gotten married at sixteen. Well, she didn't need to worry. I hadn't rushed marriage. And thanks to her for loaning me the money to buy this house in Lampton. Her interest rates were nearly nonexistent. My search for home loans had shown me exactly how much interest I could have ended up paying. It wouldn't have been pretty.

Now, I had a beautiful backyard, neighbors that waved at me and let me borrow tools, and I even had a washer and dryer inside my house. No more driving to the laundromat.

My three-bedroom, two-bathroom house wasn't a mansion, by any stretch, but it was perfect for me. If my mom and dad decided to come to visit, I had the room. If my best friend ever came back from Cancun, she planned on living with me. If I met Mr. Right, we could raise our three kids here. If I decided to travel the world, I could easily sell it or rent it out.

It made sense to buy a place like this.

That is, until I had a sudden urge to spray my neighbor's yard with Roundup. But because I was a nice person, I wouldn't do that. No, I was classier than that. He obviously wasn't, or he wouldn't have been using my garbage can.

It bothered me that I still didn't even know his name. I would have snooped through his mail by now, but he was one of those paranoid people who kept a locked mailbox. If that wasn't a sign that someone was untrustworthy, then I didn't know what was. He must have been hiding something if he was worried someone would read his mail.

With a frustrated groan, I kicked off my fuzzy slippers and pulled on my heeled booties. My white skinny jeans were miraculously stain-free when I pulled them from the wash last night. It was going to be a good day. I would choose to have a good day, in spite of my pesky neighbor. I had more important things to do than think about him.

I had a marketing team to run and a padlock to buy.

Chapter Two

KYLIE

"*B*ill in accounting wants a raise. Sheila in human resources says she's sick and tired of Trey and Marla. She's demanding you fire both of them. Tim called in sick again, and Leroy lost his glasses." I tapped my finger against my tablet.

My boss, Susan Vandenmeyer, placed her glasses on the tip of her nose. She sat behind her large, black desk, only her head visible above her large computer monitor. "They're starting early today. I'd be amused if my coffee had had time to kick in."

I pressed my lips together to keep from laughing. When I had first taken this job, Mrs. Vandenmeyer had scared me to death, but it was my first long-term position, and I wanted it to work out. The pressure from myself had made her seem even more terrifying. She was demanding, punctual, and accomplished things in an hour that would take other people all day to finish.

She also had a dry sense of humor, and now I called her Susan instead of Mrs. Vandenmeyer. She was my favorite person whenever she wasn't giving me an insanely

5

short deadline (on those days, I called her Mrs. Vandenmeyer).

"I reminded Bill that I'm the head of the marketing department, not payroll. I told Sheila if she can't handle Trey and Marla's feud, then she may be in the wrong line of work. I told Tim that a hangover doesn't count as a sickness, and Leroy is on the phone, getting a rushed order of glasses as we speak."

Susan let out a breath that, to the untrained eye, wouldn't have been noticed. But over the past year, my Susan-vision had become laser focused. It had saved me hours of work and frustration learning to read the woman.

For instance, if I didn't want her to micromanage me at a certain time of the month, then I sent her chocolates and caramel mochas.

"How is the new media manager?"

"Lyle's eager to learn." I glanced around Susan's office where we chatted every morning about that day's work agenda. The cream couch lining her wall looked like it had never been sat on.

"But?" Susan prompted.

I sat down in the high-backed chair across from her desk. "But he's not a quick learner. He's always stopping by my desk, asking questions about things he should know the answer to or things I've explained to him. He's an insecure perfectionist."

"Ah, so he'll end up being either the best media manager or the one we have to fire."

"Exactly."

"Keep your eye on him; be patient. Maybe he'll learn to start thinking for himself. If he doesn't get the hang of it by the end of the three-month trial period, we'll hire someone else. Hopefully, it's just new job jitters, or he has a crush."

"Oh, I hadn't thought of that. I may need to mention going to dinner with Landon again."

Susan didn't smile (she rarely did). "That might be the best excuse I've ever seen a girl come up with."

She was referring to Landon, my small cactus plant. I took him to dinner anytime I needed to deter an interested male.

I took Landon to dinner with me, then I would casually brag about how great dinner with Landon was at such-and-such restaurant the next time I was around the guy who had been asking me out. It discouraged most.

I didn't want to lie, which was why the minute I got my cactus, I named it and even painted the name on the pot.

Telling people "no" at work was difficult for me, so when it came to personal relationships, I didn't like to say no. Saying no was too awkward. I wanted people to like me and be my friend. Anytime you told a man no, he dropped off the face of the Earth. However, if you already had a "boyfriend," those guys usually hung around, and I could be friends with them.

Maybe my new neighbor needed a lesson in diplomacy from me. Answering the door with "I'm not looking for a girlfriend" was the epitome of self-absorbed. I could have taught him a thing or two—like the fact that not every woman he met was going to ask him out. He could stand to learn a little tact.

After I taught him basic social skills, I could tell him how uninterested I was.

I was old-fashioned. I wanted love at first sight (mutually, of course). I wanted the man to sweep me off my feet (figuratively or literally was fine). I wanted him to be dazzled by my awesomeness (but be slightly more awesome than me, because I believed in marrying up).

If I had been able to say anything coherent when he'd

been so rude, I would have rattled off my list of requirements—none of which he met.

It was frustrating how much brain space a nameless neighbor was taking up on a Monday morning. I had to start calling him Not-Hot Neighbor to remind myself that, though he might have looked good, his personality didn't match.

When I glanced up, I realized Susan was talking. I'd missed the first half of what she said. "How are we dealing with the Trey and Marla situation this week?"

"I'm going to have a serious talk with them," I told Susan. "I'll give them the new activewear company we've picked up. Maybe they'll stop fighting if they're busy working on that. They're so good at what they do, it's a shame they can't get along."

"Perhaps it's because they argue that they produce the best results. They're not afraid to step on toes."

I couldn't help but feel like she was taking a dig at me, especially with her raised eyebrows pointing at me. Then, she began typing on her computer—the sign that our conversation was finished. I stood and fluffed the pillow I'd been leaning against while I tried to think of what to say to Trey and Marla. Their constant arguing made me tired. They bickered constantly about who contributed the most to SV Marketing. Everyone liked to think they were the hardest worker.

I tried not to be petty or discriminating in these arguments, because I knew the truth. Susan contributed the most. I knew most people liked to whine about their bosses and complain about their workload (I was one of them), but Susan was scarily efficient and amazing at drawing in new clients. Sometimes, I would have liked to yell at her, but there was no question in my mind that this company was so successful because of her. It was called SV

Marketing for a reason. You didn't start a marketing company with your own initials just to let it fall apart.

Susan brought in the clients, and I ensured everything went smoothly between Susan, the employees, and the clients. I combined Susan's marketing knowledge with the client's vision. Susan had taken to calling me the mediator. It had a nice ring to it.

I liked to think that if my marketing career ever fell through, I could look into a position as a diplomat on a tropical island.

When I stepped into the hall and closed Susan's door, I could hear Trey and Marla's raised voices coming from the conference room.

Maybe I should look into that tropical island job sooner, rather than later.

———

Tuesday morning, I sat on my bar stool by my front window and peeked through my closed blinds, a large coffee cup in one hand.

After work yesterday, I stopped at the gym for my daily torture session and then ran into the local hardware store to buy a padlock. This morning, I made sure I got up an hour earlier than normal. I dragged one of my uncomfortable but chic bar stools to the window where I could watch this morning's entertainment. Three cups of coffee later, I was left feeling jittery and impatient. I intended to find out if my neighbor was using my garbage can regularly.

I was only halfway through my current cup of coffee when Not-Hot Neighbor opened his front door and poked his head outside, looking for witnesses, I imagine.

Showtime.

He glanced around as though he expected someone to

be lurking on his porch—a sure sign he was about to do something he shouldn't.

He looked at my house. I'd purposefully left all the blinds closed this morning. I had a corner of them pulled apart barely half an inch so that I could watch him. Hopefully, if I held still, he wouldn't notice me peeking through.

He stepped onto his porch with two huge garbage bags in his hands. What could he have possibly had in there? Bodies?

He was barefoot and only wearing a pair of black sweatpants as he jogged across the street. I knew I wouldn't have been caught dead out there without some shoes. Talk about picking up germs, running across a public street. Gross.

I opened the blinds a little wider as he got close to my garbage can.

I definitely wouldn't have been caught out there shirtless, but I didn't mind the view too much. Too bad I wasn't on good terms with him. I would have hired him as the face of the new activewear campaign. He made taking out the trash look good, the dirty little sneak.

He set down one garbage bag and tried to lift the lid, but it wouldn't budge. Thanks to my handy-dandy screw gun—actually, it was Dave's—I drilled a hole in the lid of my garbage can so that I could add a combination padlock to it and keep pesky neighbors out. I'd told Dave that I seemed to be having a pest problem. He was only too eager to lend me his screw gun, bless his heart.

I grinned while Not-Hot scowled at the garbage can. He grabbed the lock in his hand. He even tried to guess the number combination. He gave it a tug.

With a quick snap on the string, I raised my blinds all the way, drawing his attention toward me. I raised my coffee cup in a toast to him. His eyes narrowed, and he stomped back across the road with his garbage bags. He stopped in his driveway and tossed the garbage bags into the back of his pickup that was backed into his driveway.

I hurried to the front door and unlocked it before stepping outside. There was no way to hide my ridiculously large smile as I tried to casually sip my coffee on the porch.

He turned around and put a hand on his hip as he studied me. He scowled at me like I was the bad guy for putting a lock on *my* can. Finally, he turned around and headed inside.

That would be the last time I had to deal with my pesky, rude neighbor.

He didn't want a girlfriend, and I didn't want an overflowing garbage can.

Chapter Three

HAGEN

*I*f anyone were to have asked, I would have told them that the girl across the street was as annoying as they came. Far too chipper, smiley, and idealistic. Yes, I could tell that in the few short weeks of living in this neighborhood.

If anyone were to have known the truth, I thought she was entertaining, funny, and acted like a wet cat when she was mad. I thought those qualities were rather endearing.

I bought this house as a way to move forward with my life. I was taking the next step, even though I didn't feel like it. I planned to hang onto this and sell it in a few years, or perhaps rent it out. But after experiencing my neighbor's vengeance, I wasn't sure anyone would dare live across the street from her.

When I moved in, I had extra trash from unpacking boxes and setting up furniture. I noticed that the garbage can across the street was mostly empty, so I began stuffing some of my extra trash in there. I didn't think they'd mind.

I was wrong.

If she had asked nicely, I would have taken a trip to the

dump. Instead, she stood at her kitchen window and saluted me with her coffee mug when I tried the locked can. I knew it had nothing to do with the garbage and everything to do with the first time we met.

I may have deserved it. She'd only been trying to bring me cookies, after all.

I finished sanding the board that would soon be turned into a shelf. The old barn wood had a nice grain that would look good with a clear stain when I was finished with it. Woodworking was a hobby that I hadn't had a chance to do in a long time. It felt good to work with wood again. It was soothing. I could have solved all of life's problems while I had my hands working with my tools—which was exactly what I was doing right then: solving the neighbor dilemma and building a shelf made to order.

My favorite hobby—woodworking—was turning into a nice side business. I had enough orders for custom furniture to keep myself busy for the rest of the year. I pulled out my measuring tape to make a few quick marks on the board.

When Kylie had first knocked on my door, I'd opened it to find a woman with dark hair and a warm smile standing on my porch. Her dark eyelashes contrasted against her porcelain skin. Her lips were a pale pink, and she had expressive eyes. She was several inches shorter than me and wearing a bright-blue skirt and a white sleeveless shirt. She was gorgeous, but I had no idea why she was standing on my porch.

She introduced herself with a big smile. "Hi, I'm Kylie Boone."

That was when I remembered that my friend had been telling me he planned on setting me up with someone he knew. I kept refusing to go on the dates he set up, so he must have sent someone to my doorstep that he thought I couldn't resist—he had picked well this time.

"I'm not looking for a girlfriend," I snapped, frustrated that I would be lured in by the beauty that was standing in front of me. When I started dating again, it would be because I pursued the girl, not the other way around. I'd just come out of a relationship where the girl had pursued me. I didn't want a repeat.

The bright smile had disappeared from her face and was replaced with a grim set of her lips. Something flashed across her eyes—whether it was hurt or anger, I didn't know. Then, she'd replied, "I'm not either, but I do know there's a lake just outside of town. Why don't you go jump in it?"

Then, she turned around and marched down my stairs. It was then that I realized she had been holding a plate of cookies. Instead of climbing into a car—that I didn't see anywhere—she walked across the street and opened the door to the house directly across from me.

My stomach dropped to my feet when I realized she was my neighbor, not someone trying to date me.

She'd turned and glared one more time before slamming her door. I could have handled the situation much better. As a matter of fact, I could have been polite. Especially since it looked as though she was a nice neighbor bringing me cookies.

It seemed like I had so much extra stuff that needed to go to the dump after moving. I'd forgotten what it was like to set up a new house. I would have asked her nicely if she minded me using her garbage can, but we'd already started off on the wrong foot. I didn't want to ask a favor after I'd been so rude. I simply snuck an extra bag of garbage in here and there. I didn't think it would be a big deal.

Besides, she seemed like she was too polite to say anything about it.

She'd surprised me when she locked her garbage can yesterday morning. I hadn't expected that type of retaliation from someone like her; it had made me laugh. She was a territorial little thing. When she snapped open her blinds, she had looked so triumphant. I hadn't wanted to laugh that hard in a long time.

Then, when she stepped out onto her porch to gloat, she made me feel as though an old part of me woke up. A part I thought was long gone. I didn't want to ruin it when she had gone to so much work to frustrate me, so I made sure I scowled at her until I got back inside my house.

She'd looked so pleased with herself about her combination lock that I knew she loved a challenge. She'd looked almost gleeful at my reaction. It was like she was looking for a fight. I was only too happy to oblige her.

Chapter Four

KYLIE

*L*yle Michaelson, our new social media manager, walked into my small office with a nervous smile on his face. I was in the middle of answering emails.

It had been two days since I put the lock on my garbage, and I still felt justified about it. My garbage can wasn't even full this morning—the way it should have been when I was the only one using it.

It made me happy, dragging my garbage can to the curb early that morning. Thursday was garbage pickup day, so I unlocked the combination lock and left the can next to my curb. Not-Hot had already left for work by the time I put it out there, so I didn't have to worry about him sneaking his trash in there at the last minute. He had been filling both of our cans for the past couple weeks. How did someone make so much garbage in a week? That was what I wanted to know.

I shook my head, trying to get rid of distracting thoughts of my neighbor. Lyle was talking, and I wasn't paying attention.

"I'm sorry, Lyle. Could you start again?" I reorganized my pen holder while I waited for him to repeat himself.

"Did you like the schedule I showed you?" He straightened his crushed tie and brushed back some imaginary hairs. His thin build reminded me of a high schooler that still had a growth spurt waiting for him. He carried himself as though he wasn't sure if he should be walking on the floor.

"It looked great, Lyle. Adjust the target audience after your A/B testing, and we'll continue reaching out to influencers, but the schedule looks great."

Lyle smiled and pulled himself up to his full height. He looked as though I had nominated him for a Nobel Prize. Maybe Susan was right and he needed some time to adjust to a new job. He obviously did well with encouragement. Those million questions he'd been asking must have been nerves, because the social media campaign he'd outlined for me showed that he knew what he was doing.

"Thank you," Lyle choked out. "It means so much coming from you."

I smiled. "We always appreciate excellent work."

He shoved his hands in his pockets. "Um, are you busy Friday?"

I appreciated his initiative, but the office was officially closed on Fridays. Sometimes, Susan and I would work at the office on Fridays, but we didn't really advertise that fact. It was our chance to get stuff done in a quiet office. "Are you worried about accessing the accounts from home? I'll email you all the passwords again if you need them."

"No, uh, I have the passwords." He tugged at his tie. How he didn't hang himself every day, I'd never know. "I was wondering if you had dinner plans."

I blinked. Darn that Mrs. Vandenmeyer. Susan had

mentioned that Lyle might have had a crush on me. She was right.

Thank goodness for my cactus. "I'm having dinner with Landon that night."

Lyle looked taken aback. "Oh, I didn't know. I thought you were single."

"A lot of people think so, but Landon and I spend a lot of time together." My cactus and I were very close, especially when I didn't want to hurt someone's feelings, or ruin a work environment.

"Okay, well, I'll just go back to work then." Lyle frowned as he quickly stepped out of my office and closed the door behind him.

There was nothing wrong with Lyle. Only that he was an insecure, twenty-three-year-old kid that I wasn't interested in. I didn't want to hurt his feelings or lead him on in any way. Now that he assumed I had a boyfriend, I could go on being friendly to him, and he'd get over his little crush on me. Aunt Tricia was brilliant with the whole cactus idea.

I pulled my phone out of the drawer and texted her a quick thank-you for the hundredth time. No, I didn't have a trail of broken hearts I was leaving behind. I didn't think I should have wasted time going on dates with people I was not genuinely interested in. I knew that, someday, I would meet that person—that one person—and I'd know he was the one.

There would be stars, fireworks, and the heavens would open up for an angelic chorus.

Okay, maybe not quite like that. But I did expect to have some sort of gut feeling that he was the one. My mom knew that my dad was the one for her the moment she met him. It took Dad an hour to decide he wanted to marry her. They had four kids together and are disgustingly happy twenty-seven years later.

I planned on holding out for that type of relationship. Thanks to Landon, I was able to do that without offending people.

For the rest of the workday, Lyle kept to himself, and I left right after work to stop at the gym for forty-five minutes before I headed home.

After the gym, I made my mental to-do list on the drive home: water my hanging pots, wash my car, and pressure wash my driveway. I had noticed how dirty it was when I was waiting on Not-Hot Neighbor to test out my locked garbage can. Being the house closest to a park with a base-ball field and sand pits meant that the dust seemed to find its way to my house first.

It might have been a little sad to admit how much I loved improving my house. Instead of making friends, I was caught up in planning out my flower beds and land-scaping my backyard. My social life was pretty much nonexistent. People took energy, and when work was done, I liked to go home and enjoy peace and quiet while I did projects around my house. My house was especially quiet since it was a dead end, and there were only four houses on my street: Dave's, Karen's, mine, and the garbage thief across the street.

I turned into my driveway, but my garbage can sat smack dab in the middle of it. The garbage service was usually careful about leaving it closer to the curb. Putting the car in park, I jumped out and pulled the can next to the garage so that I had room to park.

As I walked back to my car, I noticed Not-Hot standing on his porch, watching me with a smirk. Petty as well as being a jerk. Luckily, this time he was wearing a green t-shirt with faded jeans. There were no tan abs on display to distract me.

I pulled all the way into my driveway, then gathered up a few trash items from the car. There was something amazing about sitting in a clean car every morning. It made my brain feel good. Sitting in a clean car was my version of doing drugs—it gave me a rush—which was why I immediately picked up my granola bar wrappers and coffee cup and carried them to the trash.

When I tried to open my garbage can, I noticed something. My lock was no longer there. While my lock wasn't there, a different lock was. It was a key lock, not a combination lock. I had taken the lock off before I set the garbage can out that morning so that the garbage truck driver wouldn't have to get out of his truck.

I spun around to where my neighbor stood smirking on his porch. I slammed my coffee cup and wrappers on top of the garbage can, then stomped over to enter the code that opened my garage door. It was on my to-do list to clean out the garage so that I could park my car in there someday.

As the garage door rolled opened, I watched my neighbor step off his porch and cross the street at a leisurely pace. Unfortunately, there was no need to look for cars since we were the last two houses on the street. The road wasn't a cul-de-sac, simply a dead end with a road-block sign on the end. Past the roadblock sign was a large open field that was part of the park.

I ducked into the garage and rummaged around until I found the bolt cutters I had stolen from my dad's garage when I left home. I knew they'd come in handy one day.

When I came back out of the garage, Not-Hot was standing next to my car with one hand in his pocket and the other holding a chunk of pineapple.

"Howdy, neighbor." He smirked as he took a bite of pineapple.

I narrowed my eyes and gestured with the bolt cutters. "Go away."

"Whoa," he said as he held up his hands as if I were waving a loaded gun his way. "I just wanted to come say hi. See if you needed anything."

I ignored him and began to cut the lock.

The movies made it look so easy. You need to cut through a fence to break into a top-secret facility? Snip-snip and done. Then there was me, who probably would have had better luck using a bulldozer to knock the lock off of a small garbage can.

"Maybe you should turn those the other way," he suggested as I switched the angle.

I bit my tongue to keep from screaming. How did he manage to get a rise out of me every time we interacted?

"Why don't you unlock it with the key?"

"You know darn well that I don't have the key." Something started to burn in my left shoulder as I tried to press the bolt cutter handles together.

He chuckled as he leaned his back against my car. "You know, if you asked nicely, I'd give you the key. But then again, you probably don't know how to do that."

"I don't need help from rude jerks." I put all my weight into it. It finally snapped, and I barely managed to catch myself when I tripped on my own feet.

I unhooked the lock and opened the lid to the garbage can. Dropping the broken lock inside, I added the garbage from my car before I turned around to give my neighbor a piece of my mind.

He was tossing something in the air and catching it, over and over again, as though he were having the most relaxing evening.

I took a step closer and jabbed my finger at him, preparing to tell him what I thought about him using my garbage can and changing my lock.

He pushed himself away from the car and leaned down so he'd be closer to my level. "You know, you should have just used the key."

He dangled a small key between his thumb and index finger.

I tried to make my mouth work. I really did. But I had reached the too-far-gone-and-angry point. There were a million things I should have done, but I was too busy fantasizing about running him over with my car. I stepped closer to him and did my best to look threatening. "I should stuff you in that trash can."

"You've got some steam coming out there," he said as he pointed at my head. "Have a nice day!"

With that, he jogged across the road, an evil laugh floating my way.

I closed the garage door before heading inside. After his taunting, I would just have to deal with him on my own terms.

Chapter Five

KYLIE

*H*ave you ever wondered why they have mirrors at gyms?

Let me tell you. It's all part of a marketing scheme. No one looks good after exercising. Have you ever seen someone after they climbed off the stair stepper? They look like they got caught up in a tornado. When you step off of a machine and glance at yourself in the mirror, you see how bad you look, and then you assume that you need to go to the gym more so that you can start looking good. The mirrors are simply a reminder to not cancel your gym membership.

On Fridays, no one went into the office except Susan and me. Even then, we only worked a partial day. Unfortunately, Lyle had more questions about accessing the accounts, so he stopped by the office, and I was stuck answering roughly five thousand questions. You would have thought that, as the social media manager, it wouldn't have been difficult to log into the employee portal.

I was wrong.

Finally, at noon, I told him as politely as possible that if he couldn't start figuring these things out, maybe media management wasn't for him.

I still got part of the day off, though. Three o'clock in the afternoon and I had already made it to the gym. The gym was nearly empty except for a few senior citizens and Jason, the gym rat, who was wiping down a weight machine.

That was the problem with working out earlier in the day. There weren't any young people there. I missed my chance to scout around for Mr. Right. I mean, it wasn't like Mr. Right was going to show up on my doorstep. I was going to have to put myself out there so he could find me. Which was why I usually planned my gym time strategically for when other young people were getting off of work and heading to the gym.

Maybe, one of these days, Mr. Right would decide to come to my gym, we'd make eye contact over the sea of treadmills, and know, without a doubt, that the other sweaty one was our soulmate.

It was only a matter of time before I experienced love at first sight, like my parents did. Until that time, I was going to keep coming to the gym to keep this body fit so that my Prince Charming recognized me at first sight, too.

My best friend, Carmen, thought I was insane for believing in love at first sight. I thought she was cynical. She didn't have a romantic bone in her body.

Turning up the resistance on the elliptical, I watched as Jason—who was always at the gym—helped an elderly lady climb onto a treadmill and start it at a slow pace. He even leaned the woman's cane against the wall for her.

Nice guys like that weren't easy to find. I wished I was attracted to him, because he seemed sweet and caring. He was at the gym no matter what time I was, but he didn't have that "full of himself" attitude that some men—ahem, my neighbor—had when they looked as good as he did. Unfortunately, I wasn't interested.

Two strikes on love: no on Jason, and no on Not-Hot Neighbor.

I shouldn't have let my neighbor's behavior affect me. Instead of engaging him, I should have ignored him and walked away. Oh wait, I did that, and now he probably thought that he could get away with anything. He was insane if he thought he could harass me like that.

How did you get even with a complete stranger who thought you were a joke?

By being sneaky, of course.

It couldn't be something that he could catch me doing, and it couldn't be illegal. Being raised in the Boone family meant I could come up with something to remind him to keep his big bare feet on his own property.

It only took me three more minutes of high resistance on the elliptical to come up with a strategy. With evil plans rolling around in my mind, I wiped down the machine and gathered my things.

As I grabbed my keys from the front desk, Jason met me at the door with an easy smile.

"Mind if I walk you to your car?"

I smiled at him, even though I looked like a hot mess. "Sure!"

He held the door open for me, then followed me into the parking lot. Chivalry wasn't dead after all.

"I noticed you helping that woman on the treadmill; that was sweet of you."

"That's Ethel Carver. She's been jogging every day for the past fifty years—or so she told me." He grinned and opened my car door for me. "Work been going good for you?"

"It's been good. We have a couple new employees we're trying to help get settled."

"It's always tough teaching new employees the ropes. It's probably my least favorite part of a business," he said with a grimace.

This was it. This was my opportunity to be nosy without it being too obvious. "So, what do you do?"

His eyes twinkled. "I own this gym."

"Huh." I didn't know what to say. While I'd never been accused of being observant—for example, my neighbor using my trash can for a couple weeks—you would have thought I'd have realized why Jason was always at the gym. "Now it makes sense why you're here at all hours."

He looked amused. "Did you think I lived here?"

"Yes, actually. I was beginning to wonder if you slept on the weight benches." I winked as I climbed into the car.

"I actually have a house," he said in mock excitement. "With a bed and everything. I only spend twenty-three out of twenty-four hours a day at the gym."

"I knew it. You're an obsessive exerciser."

"Ah, now you're just hurting my feelings," he said as he put his hand over his heart. "I'll try to forgive you before I see you next."

I grinned at him as he stepped back and closed my car door. He looked through the window with an attempt at a puppy-dog face. He failed, and we both ended up laughing as I drove away.

I grabbed my phone and put it on speakerphone as I called my friend, Carmen.

"Do you have any idea what time it is?" she answered.

"Yeah, I do. You're only an hour ahead of me, crazy girl."

"I was napping," her grumpy voice filtered through the line. "That's what people do on vacation."

Carmen and I had been friends since third grade. We'd even survived the awkward teenage years and cutting our own bangs together.

"Meh, you can sleep any old time. You should be out enjoying Cancun!"

"I was napping on the beach. Best of both worlds. I'm still mad at you for not coming with me."

"I couldn't exactly take vacation time when I've only been at this job for a year."

"You're annoyingly responsible," Carmen said.

"Yes, I know, but I finally got your room cleaned out this week. It's ready for when you get back."

"Perfect! I called my mom last night, and she's hiring some movers to bring all of my stuff there from the studio, but that probably won't happen for another few weeks."

Carmen lived in a studio apartment above her grandparents' garage. She spent most of her time traveling, so she wouldn't even be at the house that often, but it would be nice to have a part-time roommate, especially since she insisted on paying rent. Maybe I'd be able to knock a year or two off my mortgage with the extra income.

"How are things at work and the house?" Carmen asked. I turned onto my street. It only took a few minutes to drive from the gym to my house—one of the main reasons I chose that gym.

"I had to go into the office today. We have a new media manager, and he asks a thousand questions a day. He asked me out this week, so I had to bring up Landon."

I heard Carmen cough on the other end of the line. "Why don't you just say no?"

"I don't want to hurt his feelings!" I noticed that my neighbor wasn't home yet. I still didn't know what he did for a living. Probably took candy from children and loosened screws on wheelchairs. That would have been some-thing right up his alley.

"Kylie Boone. Grow a backbone and say no. It's not your job to protect everyone's little feelings. If you don't start standing up for yourself, you're going to be miserable the rest of your life."

"I am not miserable," I muttered as I pulled into my driveway and parked the car.

"Oh, so you like trying to make everyone feel good about themselves twenty-four seven?"

"I don't want to hurt their feelings."

"I know, but that's not what I'm talking about, and you know it. You bend over backwards just so you never have to say the word no. You're a jellyfish. I bet you haven't done a single confrontational thing since high school."

"That's not true! I locked my garbage can yesterday."

I couldn't believe she thought I was a jellyfish. Come to think of it, that might not have been a bad thing. I learned from a nature show last week that jellyfish were one of the deadliest creatures. Maybe I didn't have much of a spine, but when pushed too far, I went in for the kill. Like the time the most popular girl in school kept calling Carmen fat and embarrassing her in front of the entire cafeteria. She was a couple years older than me, but that didn't change the fact that her hair fell out with that Nair shampoo.

"What do you mean you put a lock on your garbage?" Carmen snapped.

"My new neighbor was putting his garbage in my garbage can."

"You mean the rude neighbor you took the cookies to?"

"Yeah, that one."

"He sounds like a piece of work. Wait, so you had to

put a lock on your own garbage can? I'm glad you did something. You're standing up for yourself, girl!"

I mumbled into the line as I watched out my rearview mirror as said neighbor pulled up in front of his house. He backed his truck into his driveway. He climbed out, and I could almost feel him staring at me where I sat.

"Hello? I didn't catch that. The connection must be bad."

"I said that he put a lock on my garbage can after I did. I had to use bolt cutters to get it off, and the entire time, he stood there watching and laughing at me."

Silence.

"Please tell me you didn't let him get away with that."

"I didn't let him get away with that?"

"Is that a question?"

"Maybe. I mean, really, what am I going to do, march over there and give him a piece of my mind?"

"Yes, that's exactly what you should do!" Carmen exclaimed. "Give me the story from the beginning.

I obliged her and told her about discovering my full garbage can every week and how I locked it.

"Where are you right now?" Carmen asked me.

"Sitting in my car in a pool of my own sweat."

"Is your neighbor home?"

"Yes…"

"Good. Go over there and tell him to shove off."

"Shove off? What, are we sailing?"

"Do it."

"No. He'd probably kill me and stuff me in his basement."

"Do it. You can't let people run over you like this, girl."

While some women viewed "girl" as a derogatory term, Carmen viewed it as a term of solidarity. Like she'd have your back because you were her girl. It was nice. You always knew who Carmen's real friends were based on her use of that expression.

Unfortunately, Carmen had a point. I couldn't always be diplomatic. It exhausted me trying to keep people happy. Well, today would be different. Today, I would stand up for myself.

"Fine. I won't let him get away with it. But I'm going to have to figure out what to say."

"Good. Call me after you've done it."

"Okay, will do. Got to go. Bye."

I turned the car off and grabbed my phone and bag. My thin hair felt greasy from sweat, and the majority of it had slipped from my hair tie and was sticking to my face. Before I went inside, I walked to the end of my driveway and opened my mailbox that sat next to the road. It was mainly junk mail, along with a postcard from my grandparents who were on a senior cruise. I glanced across the street and noticed the neighbor unrolling hoses in his yard. He stopped and stared at me, then slowly dropped the hose and walked to the sidewalk. He shoved his hands in his pockets and leaned against his mailbox. He must have taken a class on mastering a casual pose.

"You okay?"

I glanced around, looking for any reason why I shouldn't have been okay. I couldn't find one. "Why wouldn't I be?"

He pointed to my head. "Looks like a blender got a hold of your hair."

I growled as I slammed my mailbox shut and marched up the sidewalk into my house. I could have sworn I heard him chuckling the whole time.

It was close to midnight when I snuck outside my house and tiptoed across the street. The lights had been out for a couple hours, so maybe what I had planned *was* a little sneaky. It might have even been considered a little devious, but Not-Hot sealed his fate when he made fun of my crazy, post-gym hair.

Now I knew he had a name other than Not-Hot. His electric bill had been in my mailbox along with my junk mail.

The little trespasser had a name: Hagen Raglund.

I wasn't sure if I hated it or not. Raglund was unfortunate, but Hagen wasn't so bad. Oh well, it didn't matter if I liked it or not. He probably wouldn't be rushing to change it just to please me.

Hagen's house was a cookie-cutter version of mine: single story; sprawling, high eaves; and a large front porch. The most obvious difference was my house was creamy yellow, and his was gray-blue. I hurried to where he had set up his sprinklers in his front yard. Watching him set up the sprinklers earlier that day had reminded me how grateful I was to have an underground sprinkler system. Thank goodness for small mercies and large investments.

I picked up the first sprinkler and dragged it close to the side of his house. I knew this was where the master bedroom was. I may or may not have peeked through the windows of the house when it was still for sale.

I had a little of my mother's nosiness—no surprise there.

I pushed the sprinkler stake into the ground close to the window. It was a three-sixty sprinkler, and I made sure it would hit the window just right. I connected the hose to a Y on the faucet, then walked back around to the front of the house where there was another sprinkler.

It was the kind that you ran through as a kid. The wave

would go back and forth, and you could set it up to spray in one direction. It was the type of sprinkler childhood memories were built on.

I changed a few settings on it before setting it on his front porch. Then, I ran back to the faucet and attached the second sprinkler's hose to the Y. I cranked the faucet on as far as I could, then I sprinted all the way back to my house and sat on my front porch steps. This was a show I didn't want to miss.

The sprinkler rotated in a circle, and the loud spray hit the master bedroom window every three seconds. The timing was absolutely perfect. It sounded like a symphony to my ears, hearing the spray against that window.

Three minutes later, Hagen's front porch light flipped on. The door swung inward, and Hagen stepped outside, wearing a pair of sweatpants and nothing else, as he shut the door behind him. I watched with glee as he was sprayed with the second sprinkler I set up. He tried to shield himself from it, but it looked like he was tap dancing on the porch. Finally, he darted across the porch and away from the water's reach. I could see his dripping wet hair and soaked sweatpants from across the street.

There was a certain sense of accomplishment when you woke someone up from a dead sleep with a sprinkler and then got that same person soaking wet. I felt no remorse. He shouldn't have been so rude today. Or yesterday. Or the day before that. Or—well, you get the picture.

Hagen turned the water off, then started back around the house to the front door again. He stopped in the middle of his yard as his gaze landed on me. "You!"

His voice cracked across the empty street in the quiet of the night. Then, he started running for me. With a yelp, I scrambled up the steps and fumbled as I opened the front door. My heart was hammering in my throat, and my eyes were bugged out of my head. I hadn't thought about the repercussions of sitting outside and watching the event unfold.

I opened the door just as he bounded up my steps. I slipped inside then slammed and bolted the door. I slid to the ground on weak legs, pretty sure I'd left my stomach outside in my panic.

A fist hammered on the door and jolted it against my back. That was it. I'd have to call Carmen in the morning and tell her what a terrible idea it was to stand up for myself. Now, I was going to be dead. Killed by an irate neighbor in sweatpants.

"Open the door."

"Nobody's home!" I squeaked out.

I could hear a choking sound on the other side of the door.

"I don't know the Heimlich, so please don't start dying out there!"

"If you think I'm going to let that go, you're wrong." His deep voice shook the door and made my toes tingle.

"If you thought you could lock me out of my own garbage can, you're wrong." My attempt at an intimidating voice sounded more like a teenage mouse.

"Just wait."

I heard his footsteps echo across the porch then down the stairs. Dropping my head to my knees, I sighed with relief. I still didn't feel guilty.

*W*ork dragged by. I'd had a restless night, thanks to Kylie, and it was making me clumsy at work. It was a relief when we finally finished for the day.

As a residential electrician, my latest job was re-wiring an old Victorian house the city was fixing up as part of the historical society. Whenever we worked on Saturdays, it seemed like everything went wrong. This Saturday, we managed to find the largest mouse colony in the world.

Now, I didn't mind mice. I preferred that they were not in my house, but it wasn't a problem for me to deal with them. My coworker Jack, however, had an irrational fear of mice. When we opened up a wall to tear out the old wiring, three mice leapt out and headed straight for Jack. It took me half an hour to get him to climb out of his service van and come back inside the house.

Needless to say, after work, I headed straight to the shower to get rid of any extra mice residue. Besides, I needed to have time to plot a little revenge—no better place than a long, hot shower. By the time I walked into my kitchen, Kylie's car was home. She parked on the street, and her garage door was open. She had a pressure washer sitting in the driveway, but she was nowhere to be seen.

It was too good of an opportunity to pass up, so I slipped on a pair of tennis shoes without socks and jogged across the street. I snuck into Kylie's open garage and made quick work of shutting off the main water valve located next to her water heater. If she was going to set up a sprinkler on my porch, I was going to shut off her water. Turning it back on was as simple as turning the valve, but I wanted to watch when she came outside and turned the hose on. I jogged back across the street and opened my own garage. I'd bought a few more tools this week and they were still sitting in the toolbox on the back of my truck.

As I stood in my garage, organizing new drill bits, I heard a door slam. Kylie marched down her front steps. She was wearing jean shorts, a tank top, and some flip-flops. Not exactly the best pressure-washing outfit. Didn't she know she could tear her skin off if she accidentally sprayed herself? I'd probably done her a favor by shutting the water off. Not that she would have looked at it that way. She would've thought I was out to get her.

Maybe I was.

When she soaked me with my own sprinkler last night, I decided I'd jog across the street to have a little conversation with her. She acted like I was sprinting after her with a knife. She practically flew inside her house. Once she was behind the safety of her door, I couldn't help laughing. It was the kind of laugh that touched the depth of your soul. I couldn't remember the last time I had laughed that hard. It felt good.

I stood by my original statement that I was not looking for a girlfriend—but I was looking for a distraction. I'd had too much time by myself in the past couple months. Even I recognized my need to change some things. My mother wanted me to work things out with my ex-girlfriend. My dad wanted me to join the family business. My friend Rick wanted me to start dating again.

And my neighbor didn't want me to use her garbage can. It was such a tiny issue that it made me smile that we were both making such a big deal about it. Finally, some inconsequential thing I could pour myself into.

I took a drink out of my water bottle and watched Kylie hook the hose to the pressure washer then turn on the water. She headed back to the pressure washer and tried to start it. It took her four pulls before the engine kicked in. She pointed the pressure washer's nozzle at the driveway and pulled the trigger.

No water came out. She tapped the pressure washer with her foot—classic dad move—then pulled the trigger again.

Still no water.

I grabbed a folding chair from my camping shelf in the garage and set it up in front of my truck. I ran inside and grabbed a Coke before I sat down in the chair. Kylie was still squeezing on the nozzle when I sat down. She finally shut it off and studied the machine.

I sipped the soda and watched for the next five minutes as she tried to take apart the pressure washer, looking for the problem. When she started to unmount the engine, I figured I had better stop her before she did irreparable damage. Dave had complained to me the other day about how she always borrowed his tools, but he liked her too much to tell her no. It was probably his pressure washer.

I set the can of Coke in the cupholder and crossed the driveway. She looked up when I stopped next to her.

"What're you doing?" I asked her. I clenched my teeth to keep from laughing.

"Not that it's any of your business, but I'm trying to fix this stupid pressure washer." She tapped it with the screwdriver in her hand. Her forehead creased as she frowned.

"What seems to be the problem?" I squatted down next to her. She looked at me warily, as if she didn't trust me.

Smart girl.

"I can't get the water to come out. The motor turns on, but no water comes out. I think there's something blocking it."

"Is the water on?"

She pointed the screwdriver at me. "Of course the water's on."

Something in my face must have been suspicious, because she stood up, towering over me where I still squatted down on the concrete. Still, it was hard to be intimidated by someone her size. She was too petite.

"What did you do?" she demanded as she began unscrewing the hose from the pressure washer. She marched back to the faucet, shaking the hose. "There's no water! Why is there no water?"

She looked like she was in the middle of a seven-year drought with her dramatics. I leaned back and sat my butt on the concrete, draping my arms across my knees. This was better than TV.

"What am I going to do with no water? You!" She stomped over to me and stepped close enough that I could smell her lotion. "You did this!"

I smiled and nodded. The lotion smelled good—almost citrusy. "Yup."

Her fists balled up at her sides. She probably wanted to turn me into a grease spot that she could spray away with her pressure washer.

"Do you want me to help you?"

She sputtered at me as though I'd just offered to kill her. "No, I don't. I can take care of it myself."

"You sure you know what you're doing?"

She stomped away and pulled out her phone. "Of course I know what I'm doing. I'm an adult; I can take care of these things myself."

She put her phone to her ear and walked to her porch steps. "Hello, Dad?"

I lost it. I couldn't help it. It was a deep belly laugh from the depths of my soul. She motioned wildly for me to be quiet.

"No, Dad, that's just my crazy neighbor. Now, if I wanted to shut off the water to my house, where would I do that?"

Kylie was still holding the end of the hose. Since she was wrapped up in the conversation with her dad, I took the chance to dart into the garage and turn the water back on. Kylie shrieked, and I hurried out of the garage and started back across the street. I glanced back at Kylie who was standing on the porch, holding her phone at arms length and now had the hose pointed away from her. The front of her shirt was soaked. Strands of her wet hair stuck to her face.

"Watch your back, Hagen," she yelled at me as I ran across the street before she could spray me with the hose. She knew my name. I wondered how she found out. I knew I didn't tell her. I had a locked mailbox. But then again, I'd introduced myself to our other neighbors, and she could have easily asked them for information.

I shut my garage door and turned on the air conditioner unit. Pulling out the boards I had already cut to size, I began assembling two shelves. As I worked, I noticed my cheeks were hurting. When I reached up to rub them, I found out why: I was smiling.

It was the best kind of hurt.

After I finished with the shelves, I pulled out my sander and worked on more reclaimed barn wood. I had just turned the board over to start on the other side when my sander quit. My lights shut off, and the air conditioner was silent.

I'd lost power, and I was pretty sure it was because of a tornado. A tornado named Kylie.

Chapter Seven

HAGEN

*M*y thoughts were consumed with Kylie the rest of the week. I wished I could have blamed it on our little war. I mean, it was hard not to think about her when I was afraid for my life. Unfortunately, I thought I was catching feelings.

She had shut my electricity off. That was a gutsy move.

Things had only escalated, because to shut my electricity off, you had to be in my laundry room. She broke new territory by entering my house. Since then, I'd placed bang snap fireworks under her toilet seat. She poured vinegar into my filtered water pitcher (that was nasty when I took a big drink of water after a run). I signed her up for all sorts of junk mail that started coming yesterday. I watched with glee as she opened her mailbox and fliers spilled out onto the pavement.

For some reason, I'd been getting invites to all types of direct sales company parties. She wrote "Just Married" on the back of my truck window with some type of marker. I slapped a "Honk if you love tacos" bumper sticker on her car.

It'd been an interesting week. I couldn't remember the last time I'd had this much fun. I also couldn't remember the last time I'd looked over my shoulder so often.

It was Saturday night, and I was hosting my first barbecue at my new house. A couple friends, along with my younger brother, were coming over to see the new place. I piled the briquets in my barbecue and pulled the hamburger from the freezer. The pineapple was already chopped and on the counter.

I glanced out the window and noticed that the street was full of cars. Karen must have been having a barbecue next door, too. I pulled my keys out of my pocket and headed out to my truck. There would be more parking space on another street, but I didn't want Alex and Linley to have to walk far since they had the baby with them. Besides, I didn't mind walking. I glanced up and down the street. I could park on another street…or block Kylie's driveway.

It was an easy decision to make.

I pulled out of the driveway and parked in front of Kylie's. Just then, two more cars turned onto our dead-end street. I jumped out of my pickup and motioned for them to park in my driveway.

"Hey!" Alex yelled as he jumped out of his soccer mom van. Linley stepped out of the passenger seat and shushed him.

"Are you trying to wake up the baby?"

Right on cue, a wailing sound filtered out of the car. Their six-month-old baby girl, Mia, had the lungs of an opera singer and the stamina of a marathoner. Linley's shoulders sagged as she opened the car door and unbuckled the baby from the car seat.

The green smart car that was parked in my driveway shook as Jack climbed out.

"What are you driving, and how did you fit in there?" I asked as I crossed the street.

"It's Grandma's. My car's in the shop again, so Grandma told me I could use her commuter car," he said with a grin. We laughed because we knew the only place Jack's grandma commuted to was the local brewery. "She told me I'm lessening my carbon footprint by driving it."

Jack was roughly the size of a house. If there was a carbon footprint left behind, it was mainly because of him breathing. I didn't even want to know how he crammed his body into that car.

"Hey, are you going to be in the way of your neighbor right there?" Linley asked as she motioned to where my truck was parked.

"Nah, she's really friendly."

"She doesn't look that friendly," Jack commented. I whipped my head around and saw that he was right. Kylie was standing on the top of her steps, hands on her hips. She was wearing bright-pink shorts and a black tank top that accentuated her slim waist.

"Why don't you guys head on inside? I'm warming up the grill, and drinks are in the fridge. I need to go chat with my neighbor for a minute."

The baby scowled at me over her mom's shoulder. I frowned back at it for a couple seconds before I walked toward Kylie.

She met me at her garage door. "Move your car."

"Why don't you try saying please?"

She clenched her jaw and folded her arms across her chest. "Please, move your car."

I shoved my hands into my pockets and glanced around, loving the way she clenched her jaw as she spoke. "I don't think so."

She took a step toward me as though she could intimidate me into moving it. "I'm not kidding, Hagen. Move it."

I stepped three feet to the side.

"That's not what I meant. I'm trying to get to the gym."

"Oh, is that why you're wearing something as bright as the sun?"

"Neon pink isn't that bright."

"I thought about grabbing my sunglasses before I headed over here."

"Move the truck." This time I was pretty sure she was ready to take a swing at me. How far was too far to push your neighbor? I thought I was on the verge of finding out.

"Why don't you go for a jog? The street's full; I needed to park somewhere."

"Why don't I go for a jog? Because I don't want to be kidnapped and murdered! Why do you think I go to the gym?"

"Well, you look like you could skip a day at the gym and be just fine."

She looked surprised at my comment, then she narrowed her eyes again. "You are the worst neighbor in the world. I should have stuffed you in my garbage can before I locked it."

"You could still try."

"Don't tempt me." She turned to the keypad next to the garage door and punched in her code. 1234. She was very original.

The big door rolled open. She turned and looked at me. "I'm going to ask you one more time. Please move your truck."

I didn't want to be a jerk, but I was curious what she would do if I refused. "No. I like having it parked there."

She gave me a curt nod then marched into her garage and reached for something on top of a shelf.

I could never have imagined my ex-girlfriend acting as immaturely as Kylie and I had been. It just wasn't her style. My ex's style was money and social connections, with a side of tyranny. She hadn't always been like that, but the longer we were together, the more she became obsessed with those things—or more like her true self became more obvious the longer I was with her.

The more I withdrew from her controlling personality, the more obsessed she became with trying to run my life. She believed in cutting remarks. She never would have shut off my electricity. She never would have sprayed me with my own sprinkler. She definitely wouldn't have threatened to stuff me into a garbage can or poured vinegar in my water pitcher.

Something hard slammed into the center of my chest.

It took my breath away and knocked away any thoughts of my ex-girlfriend. Another hard something hit my left ribs, and then another hit my stomach. Thank goodness for crunches, or that one would have hurt a lot more. I looked down. Three blue paint splatters covered my shirt.

Kylie held a paintball gun aimed at me with a proud smirk on her face.

She shot me.

She shot me three times with a paintball gun. I swiped a hand through the paint, getting it good and covered, and then I advanced. Her eyes widened, and she only had time for one more shot—to my thigh—before I pulled the gun from her hands. With a shriek, she ran out of the garage. I ran after her. I overtook her in five big steps and wrapped an arm around her waist. She screamed loud enough that I was afraid she would break glass.

We'd crossed a new line. We were moving on to physical harm and the laying on of hands.

All bets were off.

"Help me!" she yelled to Alex who had come back outside to get the diaper bag from the car. "He's trying to kill me."

She tried to break free from my grasp, but she was small enough that I could easily fit an arm around her waist.

"Hey, brother, you trying to kill your neighbor?" Alex hollered.

"Not today!" I yelled back. I planted my blue hand on her cheek. My hand covered her entire face and ventured into her hair.

I released her and stepped back.

"I can't believe you wiped paint all over my face." She furiously scrubbed at her face with her black tank top, but it only smeared the paint even more.

"I can't believe you just shot me," I yelled back.

She swung a fist at me, and I barely managed to dodge it. When she started after me, I sprinted across the street.

She yelled after me, "I'm going to shove you in my garbage can, Hagen Raglund!"

I slipped inside my house and headed to my bedroom, planning to grab a fresh shirt, except Linley met me as she came out of the bedroom.

"I hope you don't mind; I laid the baby down for a nap in your bed."

"I just need a shirt."

Linley glared at me. "You can't go in there—you'll wake her up!"

With a sigh, I followed Linley into the kitchen and grabbed a piece of pineapple out of the bowl. My own niece had stolen my bed, and I wasn't allowed in my own bedroom. It looked like I'd be stuck wearing my paint-splattered shirt.

"Whoa! What happened to you?" Jack asked.

Alex butted in. "His neighbor shot him. I went out to grab the diaper bag and saw the whole thing."

It was hard to hide the grin on my face, so I stuffed another bite of pineapple in my mouth.

"Your neighbor must be crazy," Jack said.

"You're probably right about that. With neighbors like that, I'm surprised anyone lives in the suburbs." I started whistling as I washed my hands then began chopping some veggies to throw on the grill.

"So." Linley sat down on a bar stool across the island where I was working.

"So."

"So, do you like her?"

I forced myself not to react. Linley was an incorrigible matchmaker. Now that she and Alex were in the middle of wedded bliss and babies, she thought that everyone else should join them. Not that I was opposed; it was just that I had a little baggage in the relationship department, and it was closer to checked-baggage size than carry-on.

"She's different."

Linley pointed at my shirt. "I can see that. She seems fun."

"She wants to stuff me in her garbage can."

"Okay, so maybe a touch psychotic, but still fun."

"She hates me, so there's no chance she'd ever be interested in something."

"If that were true, she would ignore you. So, really, being angry at you is better than being indifferent to you."

I shrugged. "It doesn't matter. I'm not ready to date again anyway."

"Please. You're way better off without Brooke the B."

Linley never got along with Brooke, my ex. Since Linley was married to my little brother, Alex, she didn't want to have to put up with Brooke on a regular basis. She thought Brooke was pretentious and stuck up. She was right.

I thought I was failing Brooke. I thought I couldn't be enough for her—for anyone. But a few months away from her toxicity gave me clear eyes to see that she didn't love me like she said. She wanted me to be something I wasn't. I was finding peace with the fact that I was fine the way God made me. I didn't need to change. All the contempt she showed me made me begin to think that I wasn't worthy of anyone.

Now, I was reveling in the fact that she was wrong. She was the one who had shamelessly used me. It took some good friends and a crazy neighbor to help me see that. While I didn't plan on dating Kylie, I couldn't help but admit she'd brought a spark of something into my life—something that had been missing.

"Jack's barbecuing the burgers," Alex said as he walked into the kitchen.

I dropped the knife and hurried to the back door. Jack burned everything. He thought everything tasted better with a little charcoal on it. I called back into the kitchen as I opened the door. "Bring out that tray of veggies and pineapple."

"Sure thing," Alex answered.

I felt like a hostage negotiator as I tried to get Jack away from the barbecue. He finally backed away when I promised he could barbecue his own burger. Finally, Jack went inside to grab some plates, leaving me alone outside.

My phone beeped, and I pulled it from my back pocket. It was Mom texting. I swiped the screen.

· · ·

Mom: Hi dear. Your father and I are heading out of town tomorrow. We won't be back until Tuesday.

That meant I didn't have to go to Sunday family dinner this week. What a relief. It wasn't that I didn't love my family; I did. I knew they loved me in their own interesting way, but my parents were pro-Brooke and couldn't understand why we broke things off. It didn't help that Brooke was still trying to get back together, and she was using my mom to do it.

My mom loved being a grandma. Unfortunately, she only had one grandbaby to shower with love. Alex and Linley were on a marble pedestal in Mom's eyes because they'd provided Mia. They were like the star children of the family. That baby was going to be a spoiled little thing the way my mom treated her. I guessed that was what grandmas were supposed to do.

It seemed funny that my no-nonsense mother, who raised three boys and put up with zero crap while we were growing up, had already turned her craft room into a playroom for a baby that could barely sit up. Growing up, if one of my brothers or I had set foot in that craft room, we would have been in huge trouble.

My phone beeped again.

Mom: Brooke called me yesterday. We had a nice chat. Why don't you give her a call? I really think the two of you were good together.

Yet another reason I was grateful to be done with Brooke. Brooke was a manipulator and not the kind of woman who would face me down and shoot me with a paintball gun. She'd much rather stab me in the back by using people close to me.

Me: It's not happening, Mom. Let it go.

I ignored my mom's next text in favor of flipping the hamburgers, wishing that Brooke would stop coming between my family and me.

Chapter Eight

KYLIE

"Kylie!"

I looked up from where I was straightening up my desk. I tucked my phone into the side pocket of my purse and stuffed my water bottle inside. I swiped another layer of Chapstick on my lips. It had taken lots of scrubbing, but I finally managed to get all the blue paint off my face.

"Yes, Susan?"

"I'd like to speak to you in my office."

Susan disappeared down the hall. It was five-thirty, and everyone else had already left the office. Susan had always been careful to make sure everyone quit work at five so that they had time to spend with their families in the evening. It was an admirable trait that made her a considerate boss to work for. She had a great rating online for holding to a good work schedule. She valued families and personal time.

I walked through the open office door, toting my large purse with me.

"This won't take but a moment. We have a new

account that I want you to personally oversee and plan the campaign," Susan informed me with a small smile. "I would have given it to Trey or Marsha, but this person seems to think you're the only one who will do."

She passed me a small drive, and I looked it over as though I could guess what was on it. I couldn't.

"That has some information about the project on it. We have a meeting next week to discuss their marketing strategy."

"I'll start working on it this week. Anything else?"

Susan began straightening her desk and packing her purse, a small cross-body clutch. "Yes, I noticed Lyle is still hanging around your office quite often. What's happening there?"

I slouched my shoulders as I rested my heavy purse on her desk. "He's getting his work done, but he keeps interrupting my work to stop by, asking a million questions. He asked me out last week and again today. I've even used Landon as an excuse. He has trouble taking a hint."

"You'll have to be more direct with him. Next time he asks you out, tell him no. Exactly like that. No. It's a wonderful word in the English language. It's clear, concise, and leaves no room for doubt. Repeat after me: 'no.'"

I repeated the word "no" like she told me to. "I hate that word. Don't you think it would be easier to make it against company policy to date?"

"No, I don't. See? I didn't have a problem telling you no, now tell that to Lyle."

"I guess you're right; sometimes it's necessary."

"Of course I'm right. Now get out of my office. My husband's cooking lasagna tonight, and I don't want to miss out."

"Eat some lasagna for me. I have to go work out. I need to fit into my blind date dress for next week."

"Hmm, sounds interesting. Be sure to tell me all about it." I said goodbye then grabbed my bag and locked my office before I left.

The gym was packed when I got there. Little families were pouring through the gym, heading for the pool in the back. The gym opened its doors for a public family swim on Monday nights. With all the doors opening and closing because of the extra foot traffic, the gym was hotter than usual, and I didn't notice much change in temperature between inside the gym and outside when I walked to my car.

The short drive home wasn't long enough for my car to cool down. I could practically wring the sweat from my shirt, it was that wet. I parked my car and headed straight for my bathroom, peeling layers as I went. I turned the water on then stuffed my sweaty clothes in the hamper.

Finally, I stepped into my shower and let the lukewarm water cascade down my head and over my shoulders. It always felt so good to wash away sweat. Hopefully, all the sweating would help my skin glow for my blind date on Friday.

That morning, Sheila from HR told me that she had someone she wanted to set me up on a date with on Friday night. Sheila was a nice enough lady and decent at reading people. Apparently, it was a friend's cousin's nephew who recently moved to town after finishing veterinarian school.

What's not to love about a veterinarian? That should probably tell you everything you ever need to know about a man: kind, caring, smart, hardworking. We might as well head straight to the courthouse and get married.

Maybe this one would be the one. Maybe he and I would be forever, like my parents.

I sighed as I turned around to grab my shampoo bottle.

I screamed bloody murder, my feet hit a slick part of the shower floor, and I crashed to the ground. I scrambled to get up and crawled over the side of the bathtub, desperate to get away from the snake in my shower. I tried to run from the bathroom, but I slipped twice more before I made it out. I slammed the door shut and started running for the front door before I remembered that I was naked. I quickly snagged a sweatshirt and pair of shorts from the pile of clean clothes in a laundry basket on my couch. I grabbed my phone off the table next to the front door and ran outside. I was still struggling to button my shorts as I collided with a warm body.

A set of arms wrapped around me as I almost crashed to the ground.

"What's wrong?" Hagen asked.

"Sss. A sn— A ssss in my shower!"

"Geez, you're bleeding."

I glanced around, looking for blood, but I couldn't find it. "It bit me. I'm going to die!"

I didn't mind animals. In fact, I liked them, but I didn't like snakes, rodents, or spiders. Venom, bubonic plague, and poison were three good reasons why I didn't like any of those creatures. Another good reason was that my cousin Page and I stumbled upon a cottonmouth nest when we were twelve and spent far too long at the urgent care, getting treated. Louisiana had its fair share of venomous and poisonous creatures, and it wasn't unheard of for them to get inside, but I never thought it would happen to me. You expected it from cabins on the bayou— not in a house in town.

"I'm going to die," I informed Hagen in an eerily calm voice. The shock was setting in.

Big hands grabbed my shoulders and squeezed. "You'll be the first one to die from a rubber snake bite."

"It could happen; how do you know it's not poisonous?" I started babbling again as I held up my phone and started searching about the chances of dying from a rubber snake bite. I'd never heard of that kind before, but apparently, he had since he guessed what it was.

"Wait—what did you say?" I demanded. His guilty face gave him away.

He grimaced. "I'm sorry. I didn't mean for you to get hurt. I just wanted to scare you a little. Come on. You're dripping water and blood everywhere."

It took a moment for his words to register.

Now that I thought about it, the snake in my shower never moved. Its coils were perfectly round, and its eyes hadn't moved.

I jabbed my finger at his chest. "You. You put a rubber snake in my bathtub!"

A look of fear crossed his eyes as I poked him. He should have been afraid. I hadn't caught a glimpse of myself, but I could imagine what I looked like with a wet sweatshirt, dripping straggly hair, and blood dribbling down the side of my face where I hit it against the faucet when I fell.

I pulled back my finger and punched him in the chest. He flinched but didn't fall flat on the ground like I was hoping he would. Instead, he wrapped me up in a bear hug, lifted me off the ground, and carried me inside the house.

He brought me inside and set me on the kitchen counter before he rummaged through my drawers.

"Stop screaming. I'm looking for a first aid kit."

"I'm not screaming."

He turned around and gave me a look.

Okay, maybe I was screaming. Wouldn't anybody be screaming if the neighbor who hated you picked you up and carried you into your kitchen? The kitchen with knives? I watched him nervously as he neared my knife block. Now that I thought about it, I didn't really know anything about him. I still didn't know for sure if his name was Hagen. He'd never confirmed it. Maybe it was a false identity. If he decided to suffocate me, I wouldn't be able to etch his name into the floor as my final act. If you were being strangled, you only had time to write down a name. You didn't have time to write "the neighbor across the street did it."

He looked at me with a remorseful look on his face as he pulled a box of Bandaids and gauze from my junk drawer.

He stepped close enough that he brushed against my legs and began to gently mop up the blood on the side of my face with the gauze. "I didn't mean for you to get hurt."

"What did you think was going to happen?" I asked dryly.

He grinned. "I figured you'd pee your pants a little."

"I was in the shower. I wasn't wearing pants."

He began humming as he stuck a butterfly Bandaid close to my hairline. "It's not too bad. I think the shower spread the blood everywhere and made it seem worse than it is."

"You're a pain in the neck."

"Nope. I've never hurt your neck." He smirked as he put the Bandaids away where he found them.

"You're certifiable."

"Says the woman who shot me with a paintball gun."

"You look good in blue. I was doing you a favor."

He opened my junk drawer again and began fiddling with the handle.

"What are you doing? Rigging explosives?" It seemed

strange that he would try to prank me while I was watching.

"I'm fixing a loose handle while I wait for you to pass out. It'll be easier to kill you then." He winked at me then began making his rounds through all my kitchen cupboards, testing the handles and tightening all the loose ones. He used a small tool he'd pulled from his jeans pocket to help him. I watched as he worked his way around the kitchen.

"Are you trying to lure me in with kindness?"

He finished tightening the handle on my dish cupboard then stepped close to me again. He rested his hands on the counter on either side of me. I could smell his laundry detergent on him. He ignored my question. "Listen, squirt. You're not going to win this war."

"Well, now that I know murder's on the table, I just might," I replied smugly and pointed to the Bandaid.

The guilt on his face was genuine, and I would have felt bad if the blood on my face had been fake.

It wasn't. Therefore, I didn't feel bad.

"I won't need to murder you to win," he told me as he tapped my nose then pushed away from the counter and headed to the front door. "At least, I hope not."

He ducked as I chucked a roll of paper towels at him. "Don't forget to call pest control for your snake problem."

He closed the door, and I was left with a rubber snake in the bathtub and the shower still running. The water was ice cold when I went into the bathroom to turn it off. I was sure I'd have a heck of a water bill at the end of the month. Time to plot some wholesome revenge.

Chapter Nine

KYLIE

I t took thirty-six hours of surveillance and brainstorming to figure out what to do. The cut on my head wasn't very big, but it served as a reminder to get even. It was four-thirty in the morning, and I had a roll of twine that I had bought to tie up my rose bushes in the front of my house.

That flowerbed was really starting to come together.

But I wasn't worried about flowers as I untangled the twine. I was worried about revenge. I tiptoed across the street, wearing my running shoes and Christmas pajama pants. Reindeer were always an excellent choice. Besides, no one was going to see me this early in the morning. I'd have time to change out of them before decent people saw me.

I climbed up Hagen's front steps. An old, treated tree stump sat next to his front door—I was pretty sure it was the extent of decorating he was going to do on his front porch. I looped one end of the twine around it and tied it off. This was so simple it was brilliant.

Sometimes, the best pranks were the classics.

Too bad there wasn't anything to tie off the other end with. That wasn't good. You can't trip someone with only one end of your rope tied.

I glanced around. My front porch had railing all around. Hagen's did not. I couldn't tie off to the post at the front because it would have changed the angle, and he probably would have seen it. I grabbed the other end of the twine and hopped off the far side of the porch. The porch was high enough that I was able to crouch down and stay out of sight. I just had to hold the string tight around my hand—tight enough to trip him.

As I crouched down and got a close up look at my reindeer pajamas, I wondered where my life took a wrong turn. I never expected to be this immature at twenty-five. I expected to be planning my wedding, not planning a prank. I should have been learning something to enlighten myself and give me good conversation pieces when I met my dream man. Instead, I'd been searching online "how to hide a body."

The Boone family genetics were strong. That was why I had to fight it so hard. Immaturity was pretty much the strongest genetic trait in my family. It wasn't a family get-together unless my dad had told someone to pull his finger or somebody got pranked.

Moving away was a chance for me to form friendships that didn't revolve around toilet-papering someone's house. Except, you could take a Boone out of the country, but you couldn't take the country out of a Boone. Because there I was, caught in a prank war with my neighbor—and it had been fun.

That was the problem.

I'd had more fun with Hagen than I had going on fancy dates—all two of them—in restaurants, looking for love. Maybe I was just doomed to be single. Maybe those

Boone genetics ran too strong to give me a chance at finding Mr. Right. I needed to stop being so immature and focus on what was actually important to me: finding *the one.*

Just then, the front door opened, and I reflexively tightened my hold on the twine. I'd worry about finding *the one* later.

I stood up enough to where my eyes were looking straight across the deck planking. Hagen was wearing a t-shirt and shorts with a pair of running shoes. He looked good. I tugged the string a fraction tighter.

He took a big step forward.

His left foot caught on the string. He flailed his arms, trying to right himself, but the momentum was too much. He was already crashing to the porch floor. He fell with a thud. His arms spread out, trying to save his phone and water bottle from the same unfortunate fate he faced.

The sight of Hagen sprawled across his porch filled me with satisfaction. He probably wouldn't even have a bruise to show for it.

I let go of the string and sprinted out of the yard. I heard a growl. A quick glance behind me made me and my reindeer pajamas run at lightning speed. The hound of hell was behind me. His fingers grazed the back of my shirt.

How did he get up so fast?

I hurried up my porch steps, grateful that I spent so much time on the stair stepper at the gym. I slipped inside. Unlike the last time I ran away from him into my house, he caught the door when I tried to slam it.

I pushed the door with all my strength, but he muscled it open and stepped inside. My entryway shrunk as he straightened to his full height. He shut the door behind him with an ominous click. I looked around for something to protect myself with, but the closest thing was a throw pillow on my living room couch.

It would have to do. I snatched up the pillow and waved it in front of me.

"Whatever you're thinking about doing, it's a really bad idea. Really, really bad."

Hagen smirked and took a smooth step toward me. I swallowed as I tingled in anticipation.

He lunged for me.

I smacked him in the face with the pillow as he picked me up and carried me to the couch. He dropped me on the cushions then took the pillow from my hands. He held it above his head, and I crossed my arms in front of my face protectively.

"You gave me a bloody nose." He pointed at his nose.

I sat up and squinted. "Where? I can't see it."

He grabbed my shoulder and shoved me back down on the couch then proceeded to bury me under all of my couch cushions. I couldn't breathe; I was laughing too hard. It was only too obvious to me now that he wouldn't hurt me. If the worst he was going to do was stack pillows on top of me, then I was getting off pretty easy.

I heard him walk away, but I couldn't see past my lace throw pillow. He was probably letting himself out the door. Finally able to control my laughter, I sat up and straightened my pillows. Something clinked in the kitchen, and I looked to find Hagen standing at my kitchen sink, filling my coffee pot.

He hadn't left after all.

Forgetting about straightening my couch cushions, I walked into the kitchen. "What are you doing?"

"Making coffee. You look like you could use it."

There was his annoying little smirk again. I would have

argued with him, but he was right: I could have used a cup of coffee. People weren't meant to get up before six.

"What do you think of this neighborhood?" I asked as I pulled some eggs out of the fridge and cracked them into a bowl.

He punched the start button on the coffee pot. "It's been good. Everyone seems to comply with the HOA rules so far, and Karen takes her job seriously."

"She's the perfect HOA president: picky to a fault and way too much time on her hands."

Hagen nodded as he opened my mug cupboard and pulled out two cups. "Resell value will be great on this house."

"Well, I'm not planning on moving, are you?" Maybe my tone sounded too hopeful, because he narrowed his eyes at me before he pulled the creamer out of my fridge.

"I might rent it out. I've had my eye on a fixer upper in town. It'll probably go to auction in the next month or two." He passed me a cup of coffee. I waited until he took a sip of his before I took a drink. It wasn't that I didn't trust him—but I didn't trust him.

I finished stirring the eggs then scooped them onto two plates. Grabbing a couple forks out of the drawer, I handed him one.

We sat at opposite ends of the bar and ate our breakfast in silence. Hagen was sitting at my bar, eating eggs and drinking coffee. And we weren't arguing. In fact, we were agreeing about our HOA president.

I sighed and took another sip of coffee. I knew I'd wake up from this dream at any moment.

———

Sliding my purse under my desk at work, I powered my computer on. While the computer was starting up, I began sorting through some mail that was set on my desk. No matter where you worked, junk mail still found you.

I tossed the pieces of mail that were advertising prescriptions and car insurance.

My heart had finally returned to its regular rate, but my cheeks were still pink from this morning. I didn't even bother with makeup after Hagen left the house. I was too flustered, too confused. A quick swipe of mascara, eyeliner, and lipstick was all that I could manage.

I grabbed the last envelope sitting on my desk. It was addressed to me in handwritten block printing. There was no name on the return address.

I ripped it open and pulled out the paper. I unfolded it to find a typed letter.

You might not realize it yet, but you are the one for me.
  We'll be each other's forever. We'll be the ones who last.
  Signed,
  The One Who Loves You

I would have liked to say I got fan mail regularly, but I didn't.

This type of note would have been romantic if I were dating someone and he sent it with his name on it, but there wasn't a name on it, and I didn't have a boyfriend. It was more than a little creepy.

Flipping the envelope over, I looked at the address then typed it into my search bar and waited for the results. A local Piggly Wiggly showed up.

It wasn't exactly what I thought would be my forever.

Maybe it was some sort of strange marketing technique—who knows. I decided to tuck it away in a drawer. I could use it as an example of what type of marketing not to do when we hired new employees.

I put it out of my head for the rest of the day and focused on work.

I definitely never caught myself thinking about Hagen. No. Hardly at all. Only once every five minutes.

Chapter Ten

HAGEN

I had a crush on my neighbor.

I didn't know when it happened, but there was no denying it. She might have been the only woman who could have changed my mind about wanting to date again. Heck, when I got back to my house yesterday morning, I came to grips with the fact that I liked her. I *liked her* liked her. I felt like I was back in middle school. She was adorable. She made me laugh, and she had a middle school level of pranking.

We had talked. It was the first time we talked about anything that wasn't related to our little war. After we talked about our neighborhood, I froze up, even though I wanted to get to know her more. I'd been afraid I would mess everything up by saying the wrong thing. Now, I wanted another chance to speak with her.

Which is the only reason I could think of that I took the tires off of her car earlier that morning. My truck idled as I sat in the driver's seat, sipping my coffee, waiting for Kylie to step outside her house and discover my latest move.

Kylie locked her front door then walked down the steps toward her car. She opened the driver's door before she took a step back and looked at her car again. It was resting on two jacks, tires conspicuously missing.

She walked around her car, her facial expressions changing from shock to rage. *Okay, so maybe I didn't completely think this one through. I wanted an excuse to get her in the car with me. I wanted to talk with her more and didn't know how to go about it. I'd landed myself in a delicate situation, and I needed to ease her into liking me.*

It was not going to be easy.

I put the truck into drive and pulled onto the road. I rolled my window down. "Everything all right?"

Kylie whipped her head in my direction. "Someone stole the tires off my car!"

"Oh, I don't know. I'm sure they'll turn up again," I told her. *Five, four, three, two, one.* Her eyes widened as she realized what I meant. She marched toward my side of the pickup. I quickly rolled the window halfway up so that I wouldn't end up with a black eye.

"I'm going to be late for work." She frowned at me so hard that her eyebrows touched. *She was so cute when she was mad.*

"No, you're not. If you promise no bodily harm, I'll drive you to work."

She folded her arms across her chest. The blue jumper thing she was wearing accentuated her dark brown eyes. "How am I supposed to get home?"

"I'll pick you up. Think of me as your personal chauffeur."

"How do I know you won't kill me?"

"Did I kill you when I was in your house yesterday?" I inched the window down a little more.

She shook her head.

"Have I tried to kill you since I've moved in?"

She nodded.

I rolled my eyes. "The snake in the shower was an accident."

I opened the door and climbed out. She didn't run screaming for help so I took that as a good sign. I walked around to the passenger side and opened the door for her. She eyed me as she followed me around the front of the truck and climbed inside. I closed the door after her. Once I was back in the driver's seat, we made our way out of the neighborhood.

"Where do you work?"

She glanced at me out of the corner of her eye. "New Orleans. French Quarter."

I tapped the brakes a little harder than I intended. It took an hour and a half to get to the French Quarter from Lampton. I swallowed the lump in my throat. I'd brought this on myself. I'd have to call Jack and tell him I'd be late to work.

She snickered. "Just kidding. I work here in town at SV Marketing. Know where it is?"

"Yeah, I've done some wiring on that building before."

She had a satisfied smile on her face. "Bet you're glad you don't have to commute into the city."

I grinned. "You had me going there for a minute. It wouldn't have surprised me."

We rode in silence for a few more minutes, her posture slowly relaxing. Apparently, she realized I wasn't going to dump her body off a cliff. All we'd ever done was prank each other, and I wasn't sure how to cross the divide into friend territory. Except, I didn't even want to be a friend. I definitely didn't want to get stuck in the nebulous friend zone. No, I didn't want to do that either. I wanted to jump straight into being boyfriend material, but somehow, I had to do it without scaring her and without being the most annoying neighbor on the face of the Earth. I wasn't doing so good on either of those counts.

"What do you do at SV Marketing?"

She popped open her giant purse, pulled out some lipstick, and began running it across her lips. I forced my eyes back on the road. "I'mmarshingoffedector."

"I'm afraid I've never heard of that job before," I told her as I turned onto the main highway that ran through the center of town.

She rubbed her lips together before she answered me. "I'm the head of the marketing department."

"Isn't the whole office a marketing department?"

She laughed. That was a good sign. Maybe she thought I was funny. Or maybe she thought I was an idiot. Either way, hopefully it would start softening her toward me.

"It's a marketing company, yes, but there is an accounting team, a graphic design team, the photographers, social media managers, and the list goes on. I work with the ones who write up the marketing campaigns, and I also help any new employees get settled in their jobs."

"Wow. Sounds like it's an important job."

"I enjoy it." She shrugged. "I'm a little surprised I got the job with how young I am, but my boss was looking for someone who wanted to make a long-term career with SV Marketing."

I glanced at her; she did look young. She could have easily passed as a recent high school graduate. A sick feeling settled in the pit of my stomach. What if she were really that young? I didn't think age should be a requisite of love, but I didn't think I could ask someone out who was ten years younger than me. "How old is young?"

I tried to keep an eye on her and the road so I could gauge her answer. She reached toward the middle console and pulled my wallet out of the cup holder. She began flipping through it.

"I'm twenty-five," she finally replied.

I sighed with relief. No weird age gap or cradle robbing. Thank goodness.

She waved my license through the air. "Eighty-two, cross-eyed, and gray-haired."

"Very funny. It's twenty-eight." I chuckled at her interpretation of my driver's license and stopped in front of the SV Marketing building.

"You're a hundred and ninety pounds? Good grief, what do you eat for breakfast, lead?"

My truck took up two of the parallel parking spots in front. "I like to make a protein shake for breakfast complete with a few bricks for extra protein."

I turned to watch her as she sized me up. "No wonder I couldn't pick you up to fit you in the trash can. You've got me by—" She stopped herself with a little smile.

I leaned toward her. "How much do I have you by?"

She shook her head and reached forward to pinch the back of my arm. "Why is there no fat there? Everyone has fat there."

"I work for a living."

"How interesting. So do I, but I still manage to pinch some fat on the back of my arm."

She was leaning so close that I couldn't resist tapping her nose with my index finger. "I doubt that."

"No really, what do you do for a living? You said something about wiring this building."

"I'm an electrician. Mainly residential, but I'm licensed for commercial as well."

"I hadn't realized being an electrician was such a physical job. Maybe I should become an electrician. At least I'd be in shape."

"Oh, you mean these muscles?" I shamelessly flexed my forearms.

Her eyes opened wide.

"I get those from going to the gym."

"Hah! You just said you get them from working!"

"Is that what I said? I meant to say 'working *out*.'"

She glared at me, snapped her purse closed, and opened the door. "Thanks for the ride, and thanks for stealing my tires, you big narcissistic jerk."

If she didn't leave soon I was going to choke from trying to hold my laughter back. Her words had lost their bite with the twinkle in her eyes. "What time do you get off of work? I'll pick you up."

She glanced between me and the building. "Five-thirty."

Several people walking toward the building slowed when they saw Kylie standing next to my truck. They must have been her coworkers. Kylie shut the door and hurried after them, casting a nervous glance over her shoulder in my direction, as though she were worried I would embarrass her.

I always did hate to disappointment people.

I rolled down the passenger window. "Have a great day at work, honey pumpkin!" I hollered after her.

Her coworkers laughed, and Kylie turned to give me her death glare with bright-red cheeks. I smiled at her and blew her a kiss. I knew she'd make me pay for it later—and I couldn't wait.

———

I was getting nervous thinking about picking Kylie up from work again, and I was rehearsing all the different topics of conversation we could have. Conversations weren't easy for me unless I was talking about something I loved. Social get-togethers made me feel like I was being tortured. Kylie was different.

I came up with some options as conversation starters for the drive home: What did she think of the trend in real estate in our area? What did she think of the last Harry Potter book? Was she as obsessed with baseball as I was? Did she like dark or light turkey meat? I needed to find out the answers to these important questions so that I would know how to proceed. Because who prefers light turkey meat over dark? It's an abomination.

My excitement continued to grow until three-thirty when I got a text from Brooke.

Brooke: We need to talk. I made us reservations for dinner tonight.

Me: No.

Brooke: No, that time doesn't work for you? I talked to your mom. I know you don't have plans tonight.

Me: Just no.

She sent a few more texts that I ignored while I worked, and I finally had to put my phone on silent. It made me angry the rest of the afternoon, but that was Brooke for you. She didn't ask things; she demanded them. If you didn't perform to her satisfaction, then she threw a fit.

When I picked Kylie up from work, all of my brilliant conversation starters were forgotten as I mulled over Brooke's texts. The moment I'd been looking forward to all day was overshadowed by a woman who shouldn't have had a hold over my life anymore.

Kylie and I said about two words before she asked me

to drop her at her gym. I asked her what time I should pick her up as I stopped in front of the entrance, but she motioned at a man standing in the front window and told me that he would give her a lift home. She pulled a pair of tennis shoes out of her giant purse as she walked into the gym.

She didn't even look back.

I drove home in an even darker mood than when I left work—I'd forgotten to ask her dark or light.

When I backed into my driveway, I didn't even have the energy to do any woodworking. I rolled Kylie's car tires out of my garage and put them back on her car before I took a thirty-minute shower. I got out of the shower, pulled on a pair of shorts, and turned on the TV so I could zone out and eat chips. I didn't want to think about Brooke or how I was messing up my chance with Kylie.

When I stood up to grab a soda, I glanced out my front window to see an unfamiliar car parked beside Kylie's. A man stepped out and walked around to the passenger side. He opened the door, and Kylie stepped out.

It was the same man Kylie had pointed out to me at the gym.

I growled.

He was even a gentleman. I stepped close and opened my curtains a little wider. Neither of them noticed me as they stood on the sidewalk, talking to each other.

After what felt like hours to me, the man leaned in and gave her a long hug then bent down and kissed her head.

I couldn't watch anymore. I wished I could have blamed the sick feeling on the chips, but I thought most of it was due to the fact that Kylie already had herself a nice guy. A guy who opened her doors and didn't use her garbage can. A man that didn't put a rubber snake in her shower or shut off her water. A man that kissed her like a gentleman. Because I knew that wasn't how I would kiss her if I ever got the chance.

I flopped, stomach down, on my couch and shut off my phone. There were five new texts from Brooke, and I wasn't in the mood to read them.

Chapter Eleven

KYLIE

I couldn't ride in Hagen's truck again. It was too much—too confusing—to be in such a small space with him.

I was getting too attached.

That was why I told him that Jason would give me a ride home from the gym. I didn't know if that was true or not, but I did know that I couldn't be in a confined space with Hagen again. My brain was getting wacky ideas. It was telling me things that didn't make sense, like "Hey! Look! The big jerk of a neighbor you're trying so hard to hate is actually funny, kind, and he works hard."

As if I needed that lethal combination to be something he had. I wanted to be annoyed by the guy. He'd been so rude to me when I first met him. He'd been nothing but a pain in the butt ever since, but I'd had a blast with him. War with him had made me feel alive.

Unfortunately, Hagen was one hundred percent not interested in me. Yet, that brain of mine was still getting funny ideas that said, "What if... What if he could be more?"

I needed to stop that right there. It hadn't been love at first sight, and it was probably my lonely self just looking for someone—anyone—to be interested in. Why couldn't it have been Jason?

Oh, that's right, we friend-zoned one another when he drove me home after my workout. We'd both expressed how much we liked each other—as friends. We even decided to play tennis on Sunday afternoons. It actually helped calm me after the day I'd had. I needed to know I had a friend. Maybe Jason would be able to provide me with some insight into the rare and confusing thing called the male mind.

As Jason pulled up in front of my house, I noticed Hagen had already put the tires back on my car. I made a quick note in my phone that I needed to learn that particular skill set.

Note to self: Learn to change tires on my car.
Note to self: Learn to play tennis.

Jason opened my car door for me then gave me a big hug, telling me he was glad we could be friends. He even waited until I was safely inside my house before he drove off.

I pulled my phone out and called my mom as I stared out my front window at Hagen's house.

Four rings later and my ten-year-old brother, Tatum, answered the phone.

"What do you want?"

"Hello to you, too. Could you hand the phone to Mom, you little brat?" I love my family, I really do, but Tatum is the spoiled baby of the family. "When are you going to come visit me?"

"Did you get a dog yet?"

"Not yet."

"Then I don't want to visit you. Call when you have a dog. Mom doesn't want to talk to you unless you have a dog either."

"Mom doesn't care if I have a dog or not. Give her the phone, Tatum." I pulled the phone away from my ear when Tatum yelled for Mom. She was probably making dinner.

"Hello?"

"Hey, Mom, is it a bad time?"

"No, sweetie, it's taco night. I'm just stirring the meat."

We chatted for a few minutes, and she caught me up on all the latest news at home. She told me about the summer baseball camps and how excited Payton was to be a freshman in high school.

"How are you doing, sweetheart? Dad said you were having some water trouble the other day. Is everything all right?"

"Yes, it's fine," I told her as I walked to my mailbox and grabbed the mail. I headed back inside as I sorted through it and debated what to tell her.

"Any boys you want to tell me about?"

I was pretty sure Mom was going to call anyone my age "boys" or "girls" for the rest of her life. She was in that permanent mom mode. She mothered anything she could get her hands on.

"No boys. I'd had a blind date scheduled, but today at work, I found out that he already met someone this week."

"That's too bad. There's no one else on the horizon?"

"Nope. No love at first sight for me yet. The most excitement I have is with my pesky neighbor."

"You mean Dave, the one who lets you borrow his tools?"

"No, I mean my new neighbor across the street who's driving me crazy."

"Tell me."

I spent the next twenty minutes venting to my mom about Hagen. By the time I finished, she was silent.

"Anyways. Other than that, life's been going good here."

Mom cleared her throat. "What does this neighbor look like?"

"He's disgustingly good-looking. If only he had a nice personality to go with it."

"Aha."

I stopped tapping my fingers on the counter. I'd told her too much. It was never a good sign if Mom had an "aha" moment. "Something on your mind, Mom?"

"Is there something you would like to tell me? Like the fact that you like this new neighbor of yours? And that he likes you too?"

"Mom. You're crazy. I don't like him. He obviously doesn't like me either. Didn't you hear anything I just said? He drives me crazy!"

"Hmmm, that's interesting, because your father used to do the same thing—still does."

"You told me it was love at first sight."

"It was. But it doesn't mean I didn't want to kill him sometimes. Honey, that's part of getting to know someone. I think you have more of your dad in you than you think, and it sounds like your neighbor has just as much crazy as you do."

"No, you're wrong about that. He has a lot more crazy than I do. You really think he might like me?"

"Boys have been annoying girls for attention since the beginning of time. If he wasn't interested, he never would have replaced that lock on your garbage can. He especially wouldn't have arranged it so he could drive you to work."

Maybe he just needed a distraction. He'd seemed especially uptight when I first met him. He was probably using me as an interesting way to pass the time.

"What did Dad drive you crazy about?"

"Anything he could. Even though he annoyed me sometimes, I still thought he was the sexiest thing I'd ever seen."

"Mom. That's gross."

"Why do you think we had four kids?"

"Gag! I'm going to go bleach my mind now. Thanks for that."

"Love you."

"Hah. Love you too, Mom. Have a good night."

"Okay, sweetie. Call me when the neighbor asks you out."

"Not going to happen, Mom."

She just laughed and hung up.

I grabbed the last piece of mail that was hand addressed to me. I ripped it open.

You are everything to me.

That was it. No signature.

I looked up the return address on my phone. It was the same Piggly Wiggly that sent the note to the office. I swear they hired a middle schooler.

I left the note on the counter while I made dinner. I was still confused by the drive with Hagen today. It was stilted conversation at first, but then we seemed to find a groove. Our good-natured teasing was fun. I owed him one, especially since he was the one who took my tires off my car.

Yes, it was a dirty trick, but it was a calculated one, too. He usually left for work before me, which meant he waited around to give me a ride to work.

There was only one thing I could have done: get even with him for taking the tires off my car.

———

If Hagen thought I would let the whole tire removal thing slide by just because he gave me a ride to work, he was wrong.

Do you know what it's like to watch a man pull out of his driveway with a garbage can chained to his truck bumper?

Because I did.

Chapter Twelve

KYLIE

$\mathcal{T}$he new campaign Susan had me working on was for a local gym. Susan wanted us to keep an open mind while brainstorming our work, so she never told us which business we would be working with during the initial brainstorming period. This lasted usually a week or two before we had our first meeting with the client. She wanted our "creative juices flowing without prejudice." I guessed it made sense. If it was a business you weren't crazy about, you probably wouldn't have felt like using your best ideas for it.

By the time I finished up at the office on Friday, I had more ideas for the gym that I wanted to lay out on paper at home. I was old-fashioned like that, and I was way more creative on paper than I was on a laptop or tablet.

After work, I skipped going to the gym and, instead, headed straight home. The only stop I made was for some chocolate-peanut-butter ice cream at the store—because if you were going to skip the elliptical, you should have a good time doing it. I was feeling a little down about not going on a blind date tonight. I knew people always dreaded blind dates, but if I didn't go on a date, how would I ever find my soulmate?

When I got home, I shuffled the bags of groceries—because I was incapable of buying only one thing at the grocery store—to one arm so I could unlock my door. I unlocked and opened it.

A tornado must have touched down in my neighborhood because the inside of my house was a disaster.

My living room was trashed. Magazines were thrown across the room. The bookshelf was tipped over onto the living room floor. Some of the books were thrown about the room. Pieces of Landon laid scattered across my living room floor. No cactus deserved that type of death.

Couch cushions were on the floor next to the kitchen bar.

My heart skipped a beat as I took in the disaster that was my house.

Someone had broken into my house.

I set the groceries on the ground then opened the coat closet. As I pulled out my baseball bat, I heard a thump come from the back of the house as I crept toward the hallway. Something crashed in the laundry room, and then the back door slammed. I peered inside the laundry room. The back door was still shaking as if someone had slammed it.

Someone had been in my house. Someone was in my house when I got home. My heart prepared for takeoff. I fumbled to pull my phone out of my pocket to call the police.

Who would—

I forced my mind to stop flailing around. I ran to my room. My laptop was still there. My tiny TV still sat in the living room.

My ancient iPod was still there. There was nothing

missing. Whoever had done this hadn't stolen anything of value. I didn't have much of anything that was valuable, so maybe the thief had assumed I'd have some nice things. I lived in a nice neighborhood; they probably thought I owned expensive electronics or maybe nice jewelry.

I glanced out the living room window toward Hagen's house.

That was when I realized the truth: Hagen had done this.

This was because I tied the garbage can to his truck and he pulled out without noticing. Sure, it had strewn garbage everywhere, but that wasn't even close to the amount of destruction that he had done to my house.

Our pranks had been escalating for some time now, but this was too far. What would happen next? Would we kill each other? I'd already shot him with a paintball gun. What could stop me from shooting him with a real one?

I knew one thing was for sure. I had had enough. I couldn't believe I had let this little tiff go this far. Now I remembered why I had wanted to squash that Boone immaturity.

Before I banned all of my Boone heritage, though, I was going to tear his head off. Then, I was going to make him pick up the mess he made of my house.

I opened my front door and marched across the street.

Knocking on Hagen's door with my baseball bat, I could hear country music coming from inside.

Uncultured Philistine. There were three unfamiliar cars parked in front of his house and in his driveway. Maybe his friends had helped him trash my house.

If he didn't make this right, I was going to call the police.

I wished I had taken the time to change out of my work clothes. My navy high heels were pinching my toes, and my short yellow skirt and navy sleeveless blouse didn't seem very intimidating—and I wanted to look intimidating. What kind of clothes did scary people wear? I wasn't sure. I'd have to research that.

The door opened.

Hagen smirked as he looked me up and down. I knew the moment he realized I was carrying a baseball bat. His eyes widened, and he started to swing the door closed, but I threw out an arm and pushed it open again. Seeing his panicked look made me feel better.

I marched inside and slammed the door. It was only the second time I had stepped foot behind enemy lines, but I was too focused on the jerk standing in front of me to pay attention to his lair.

"You've gone too far this time." I gestured at him with the baseball bat. "This is it. We are done. If you even look at my house, I will call the cops. If you set foot on my lawn, I will taser you. If you even think of using my trash can, I will stuff you in it!"

He cleared his throat and wrapped his hands around the baseball bat that was poised at his chest as though it were a sword about to pierce his heart. Not a bad idea, actually. I'd have to call Great-Uncle Arnold and see about borrowing a sword from his collection.

"First off, if I'd known you would be this upset about it, I wouldn't have done it. Second of all, I don't think I would fit inside your trash can." Then he smiled—like it was completely normal to destroy your neighbor's house and then accuse them of overreacting.

"My couch! My favorite coffee mug! Landon! My drawers! I heard you slam the back door just now. You probably broke something in the laundry room. How did you sneak back so fast?!"

I pointed back and forth from my house to him with

my baseball bat. He looked at me with a confused look on his face. "Wait. You think I was at your house just now? I wasn't!"

I snorted. "At least if you're going to do something, take credit for it."

He took a step toward me, and I stepped back against the front door. He was looming again. I didn't like it when he loomed. It was too distracting. It made me all too aware of how attractive he was.

I poked him in the chest with the bat. "This little war is over. Trashing my house goes beyond a practical joke."

He snatched the baseball bat from my hand and grabbed my arm. This must be the part where I got murdered, so I did the only acceptable thing. I screamed. Loudly. Maybe Dave would hear me and come help.

Hagen grabbed the back of my head, and I got a mouthful of his cotton T-shirt as he slammed my face into his chest.

"Be quiet, the babies are napping."

I swallowed a scream and tried to remove my face from his hard chest. *Did he say "babies"?* He must kidnap small children as a side hobby to terrorizing the neighborhood. How diversified.

"You have a baby? What house did you take it from?"

He stepped back enough for me to look up at him, but he kept an arm around my back. "It's not my baby; it's theirs." He jerked his chin to the side.

In my heels, I was tall enough to see over his shoulder —just barely. Sure enough, we had an audience to our little heart-to-heart. Lovely.

A couple in their thirties sat on the couch, holding hands, a baby asleep in its carseat next to them. Another man was standing by the back door, holding a beer. A third man sat at the bar, eating a sandwich. Another woman sat in Hagen's recliner, rocking a sleeping baby. They all looked equally amused by the local impromptu theater.

"Same time next week," I said before I spun around and tried to open the front door.

I didn't even make it past the doorframe before Hagen grabbed my hand and pulled me back inside.

"What happened to your house? I wasn't in your house just now. Ask anyone here."

He spoke quietly, and I glanced over his shoulder to make sure his guests couldn't hear. They had all turned back to their conversations and the game on TV.

I looked back at Hagen's green eyes. He looked concerned. I swallowed the lump in my throat.

"You mean, you didn't run out of my laundry room and slam the back door ten minutes ago?" I whispered.

Hagen's lips formed a hard line. Gone was the semi-permanent smirk when we were sparring. Now, it was replaced with a focused look as he slowly shook his head.

I closed my eyes and let out a breath as I realized what he was thinking. "Someone broke into my house."

"Who ran out your back door?"

"I thought it was you." I licked my lips so that I could speak again. "They were still in the house when I got home."

Hagen blew out a breath before he wrapped his arms around me. I hadn't realized I was shaking until his arms surrounded me. It felt good...safe.

"Thank God you're alright. You could have been hurt! Why do you have a baseball bat?"

"My first thought was that someone had broken into my house, so I grabbed the bat. Then, I figured that you were the one who did it." I gulped. "Except, someone did break into my house, and I got home before they were done."

Hagen stepped back then wrapped his arm around my shoulders and guided me into the living room.

"Hey, Rick, someone broke into her house. Do you want to make the call?" Hagen said to the man sitting on the couch next to a tall, beautiful woman.

The man stood up and pulled a cell phone from his pocket at the same time. His face was grave as he held the phone to his ear. No one spoke, but someone muted the TV, and the country music shut off.

Rick stepped into the kitchen, and he spoke quietly into the phone. The woman who'd been sitting in the recliner came to stand next to me and shifted the baby-bundle to one arm. A dark, curly head rested on her shoulder.

She touched my arm. "Are you okay?"

I tore my eyes from the sleeping infant in her arms to the soft smile on her face. "I think so. I don't think they even took anything, so that's good."

"I'm sorry. Even if you're not missing anything, it's scary knowing a stranger was in your house. I'm glad you have Hagen here."

Hagen's arm tightened around my shoulder. He was looking at me with those warm, green eyes again.

Now I felt guilty for assuming that he had destroyed my house. We might have been crazy, but I was definitely the more destructive of the two of us.

"They're sending a couple of officers. I told them you would wait here with me," Rick said as he stepped back into the living room.

Hagen explained, "Rick's a detective in town. He'll make sure they do everything they can."

I tried to stiffen my legs to fight the shaking, but it only made it more exaggerated. Hagen squeezed my shoulder.

"I don't know why I'm shaking."

"You chased a burglar out of your house in high heels.

Anyone would be shaking after that. I've heard it's a workout just to walk in heels." He winked at me as he led me to the couch and gave me a gentle push. When he wasn't trying to make me mad, he could be pretty sweet. Not to mention, picturing him trying to tiptoe around in heels would make anyone smile.

"Now, you sit there, and I'll bring you something to drink while we wait."

The woman holding the baby sat down next to me. "I'm Linley."

I reached out to grasp her extended hand. "Kylie."

"This is Kara." She motioned to the woman on the other side of me.

Kara said, "I'm so sorry you have to deal with a break in. Does anyone else live with you?"

I shook my head. "No, just me."

"Don't worry, Rick's good at his job. I'm sure they'll catch the person soon," she said as she patted my hand.

For the next fifteen minutes, Linley and Kara did their best to draw me into conversation and distract me. It didn't work, but I appreciated the effort, and I found myself getting invited to girls' night—something I actually looked forward to, even though I didn't know them at all.

I guess something good came of it, after all.

Chapter Thirteen

KYLIE

*I*t took the police five hours to arrive. Actually, it was probably only like five minutes, but it felt like an eternity. All that I could think about was the fact that I almost confronted a thief with a baseball bat.

By myself.

It seemed like a good idea at the time, but the officers who questioned me didn't agree. The police made sure I knew just how dangerous that could have been. Yes, thank you, officers of the law, for pointing out that I could have been dead, but all I wanted to do was eat my chocolate-peanut-butter ice cream when I got home. I didn't expect to hang out in my house with a burglar.

When they asked if I knew of anyone who would want to cause me harm, I felt like dialing a private security firm. Maybe if I maxed out some credit cards, I'd be able to afford a bodyguard. I had missed a lot of details that the police had found. Some of them were details I wished I never knew about, because the chances of me ever sleeping again were zilch.

The burglar had written the word "Forever" on the

wall above my bed. The police officer who was filling out the report wanted to know if that word meant anything. I told him it meant I would be moving to Alaska.

He laughed. He didn't realize I was serious.

I mentioned the strange notes that had come to my office and my home, but they brushed it off as coincidence. I didn't quite believe them, though they offered all sorts of helpful advice about how to keep my home safe from intruders. The only thing I remembered from their talk was that they said that the back door was jimmied open and that I should add a chained bolt to it.

When the three police officers left—though they were sorry they couldn't do more—they left me with numbers to their direct lines in case I needed anything.

I asked the older detective, Jim, if I could keep him forever, but he said his wife and kids would miss him eventually. He said that I had a good neighbor with Hagen looking out for me.

The neighborhood seemed unusually quiet after the three police cruisers left. Rick took his wife and baby home after he, too, gave me his personal cell number to call if there was any trouble. His wife gave me a big hug and told me she'd help me clean things up in the morning. She seemed so sweet and kind even through the craziness going on around me.

That left only Hagen and me when I walked back into my house. It felt far more menacing now that I knew it wasn't a prank gone wrong.

I walked into my bedroom with Hagen right behind me. I didn't know why I hadn't noticed the word written on the wall when I first looked around my house. He'd used my own permanent marker to do it. The pen had been tossed onto my white pillowcases.

I'd have to wash everything in this room before I could go to sleep tonight.

I watched as Hagen grabbed a bag from inside my closet. He snatched some clothes from my dresser and shoved them into the bag. Next, he snagged my phone charger from the wall—it was one of the few things that hadn't been thrown across the room.

He left the bedroom, and I continued to stare at the wall.

I jumped a few feet when he came back into the room.

"Come on." Hagen grabbed my hand.

"What do you mean?"

"You're not staying here tonight. You're sleeping at my house."

"Of course I'm staying here. This is my home!" I tried to laugh, but I didn't like the hysterical tone that crept into my voice. To be honest, I didn't want to stay the night at my house, either, but I didn't know Hagen other than the little war we had going on. Yet, he stayed by my side and held my hand while the police searched the house. It was comforting. It made me like him even more, but then he had to go and get all cranky again.

Hagen stepped in front of me and looked me in the eye. "Don't argue. I want you to be safe."

"I don't even know you, other than you're creative and have a horrible need for revenge. You could murder me in my sleep." My excuse sounded feeble, even to me.

"The back door is hanging off its hinges. You're not staying here by yourself."

Before I had a chance to argue, he tugged on my arm and dragged me through my house, out the front door, and across the street.

I tried to tug my hand free, but he had a firm grip, and I was still wearing high heels.

By the time we were in Hagen's living room, I was plotting ways to maim him.

He made me sit on his leather couch and pointed a long finger in my face. "Stay."

He set my bag next to me and headed to the kitchen.

I would have made a golden retriever proud. I didn't even twitch a muscle. Because now that I was here on this comfortable couch, I didn't want to leave. I was perfectly happy to stay with a good-looking man who wanted to keep me safe from scary people who wrote words on my wall.

When he came back into the living room with a bag of chips and some soda, I knew for sure I wasn't leaving. If that wasn't marriage material, I didn't know what was.

On principle, I should have said something snarky. I didn't want to encourage caveman behavior. (Because if you're dragging someone around against their will, you're a caveman—not a hero.) But right now, I'd rather stuff my face with chips.

Hagen grabbed the remote and turned on the TV. He flipped to the history channel. It was like, secretly, he was a hundred years old. Even worse? I was perfectly fine with his choice. I wanted to sit there and learn about the history of cotton mills in northern England. It sounded thrilling.

I laid my head on the arm of the couch. Hagen got up and disappeared down the hallway. He came back carrying a fleece blanket. He tucked me in then sat in the recliner again.

He might have been hero material, after all.

Chapter Fourteen

HAGEN

I left the TV on even though Kylie was asleep. I hoped having some background noise would be soothing to her.

I hoped I'd done the right thing by bringing her to my house. When I saw her look of terror as she stared at the word written on her wall, I knew I couldn't leave her there by herself. I planned on calling an alarm company in the morning and adding another chained lock to each of her doors. Kara texted and told me she would send a cleaning crew at noon.

If Kylie wanted to stay in her house by herself, then I was going to make sure she was as safe as possible. The sergeant told her that the perpetrator had probably learned her routine before he broke in. That didn't sit well with me that someone had been studying her habits.

Kylie's phone chimed where it sat on my coffee table. I glanced at her, but she didn't stir. I picked it up. It read "Mom" with a heart emoji. I debated on waking Kylie up and asking if she should call her parents, but she looked so peaceful that I didn't have the heart to.

I unlocked her phone—she didn't bother to have a password.

Mom <3: Hi sweetie! Your dad and I are getting ready for our anniversary trip. Just wanted you to know we'll be leaving early tomorrow morning and the kids will be staying with MiMi. Love you!

As I was debating whether or not to call her mom, the phone lit up with a call from "Mom <3." I answered.

"Hi, honey!"

I cleared my throat. "Um, hello, you don't know me, but—"

"Is Kylie alright?" the voice shrieked across the line. "Come here, Todd! A strange man answered Kylie's phone!"

This wasn't good. I wasn't easing anyone's worries with this. I reached down and hit the FaceTime option and waited for a few seconds as it connected. Kylie-in-twenty-years filled the screen. A man's face crowded in. That must have been Todd.

"Who are you?" he asked.

"I'm her neighbor."

"Oh, you're the disgustingly good-looking neighbor. I'm Rose." She smiled.

Todd scowled, and then his face smoothed out. "Are you dating my daughter?"

I leaned back from the phone and sat up straight. "No."

"Well, why not?"

Not exactly the question I was expecting. "Because I don't think she likes me much."

"But you have her phone," her mom interjected.

"Yeah, about that…" I gave them a quick rundown of what happened with the break-in and watched their faces change from disbelief to horror, and then Todd disappeared from view.

Rose called after him. "Put the gun away. No, you are not driving there tonight. Come back here and sit down."

I couldn't help smiling at the one-sided conversation, glad that Kylie had parents who worried about her.

I flipped the screen around so they could see Kylie sleeping on my couch. "I didn't want her to be home alone tonight, so I brought her over here to stay. I'll call an alarm company in the morning, and a friend is sending someone to get the house straightened up so she won't have to worry about it."

"Thank you for keeping her safe," Rose said as she pressed a hand to her chest. "We'll cancel our trip and be down there as soon as we can tomorrow."

Todd didn't say anything, so I took it as my chance to speak. "Nothing was taken out of her house, but the whole place was trashed. It was as though they were looking for something. Since they were interrupted, I'm worried they'll be back."

Todd nodded, and this time, Rose was standing up and walking off with the phone in her hand. I heard the jingle of keys before the screen jerked around and Rose was sitting down, arguing with Todd that she was going to drive down here tonight.

Todd steadied the phone. "Look, I don't know what's going on with you and Kylie, but I doubt Kylie has been passive in this little war of yours."

I shrugged. "She shot me with a paintball gun and gave me a bloody nose."

Todd nodded like it was the most normal thing in the

world. "She's definitely the calm one of the family. Now, Rose and I are getting ready to go on our trip for our anniversary. I'd like to still go, but I'd need your help."

"What can I do?"

"Would you mind letting her stay with you for a couple days? I'll send someone to stay with her, but it might take a day or two for them to get there since they'll need to take time off of work first."

"Yes, that's fine. She might not be real happy with that, but I'll keep her safe."

We chatted a little while longer. I learned they were going to San Diego for their anniversary trip and that the kids were staying at the grandparents'. They even told me some embarrassing stories about Kylie that I would be saving to use at a future date. I talked about my family and my job to help put them at ease and know that I didn't moonlight as a serial killer.

With a promise that we would talk soon, they hung up, and I had a chance to get some sleep. I slept in the recliner, afraid that if I went to sleep in my bed that Kylie would wake up and forget where she was.

The next morning, I woke up early with a kink in my neck. My recliner was perfect for binge-watching sports and the history channel. It wasn't perfect for trying to get a good night's sleep.

Standing up, I popped my back and glanced at the couch.

Kylie wasn't there.

Quickly searching the house, I found her asleep in my bed, still wrapped up in the fleece blanket I had tucked around her last night.

As quietly as my mom sneaking chocolate on a diet, I shut the door then headed to the kitchen to cook some breakfast. We were caught up enough on work that I didn't need to work on a Saturday. I texted Jack to let him know I wouldn't be working today, but if he needed some more hours, he could head in. I asked Alexa to turn on today's hits and pulled some bacon out of the fridge and pancake mix from the cupboard.

I'd never cooked breakfast for someone else before. This was new territory. The box of pancake mix had been a companion of mine for eight years. It was a dry mix, so it couldn't possibly go bad.

I followed the directions and fried it in a skillet next to the bacon, dancing to the music while I flipped the pancakes.

"Something smells good." Kylie stepped into the kitchen, and I immediately stopped dancing. She'd had enough frightening experiences; she didn't need to add seeing me dance to the list.

She grabbed a few pieces of bacon off the plate I held out to her, then she sat down at the bar. I poured her a cup of coffee, adding some creamer to it. I remembered she liked it sweet from the last time we had breakfast together. She whispered "Thank you" and sipped the coffee and nibbled the bacon. I stood there, mesmerized, watching the messy-haired girl sitting at my bar. Dark hair tumbled around creamy skin, her cheeks still rosy from sleep.

Something started smoking, and I realized I'd forgotten about the last pancakes in the pan. I grabbed the pan and dumped them onto a plate. The underside of the pancakes were completely black. At least the first couple batches I'd cooked had turned out decent. Kylie snickered behind me, but when I turned to glare, she stuffed an entire piece of bacon in her mouth.

"Not a word from you, Snow White," I told her.

She shoved another piece of bacon in and shook her head. She looked like a chipmunk and she was still cute.

"You know, it's okay to breathe in between bites of bacon." I grabbed a few pieces for myself while I dug around in my fridge for some syrup.

"It's bacon," she said. "It's never okay to take a break."

Grinning, I put together two plates of pancakes and passed a plate to her. There were three barstools, and she sat on the middle one, so I sat down to her right.

I watched as she took a bite of the pancakes and chewed—and chewed. Her forehead scrunched up as she kept chewing.

That wasn't a good sign.

I took a bite of my own pancake and had the same problem. It was like I had cut up my work boots and tossed them in a pan. I spit the bite out and snagged both of our plates to toss them in the trash.

"That was bad."

I turned around to see Kylie had her head resting on her arms, her shoulders shaking. The pancakes had sent her over the edge. I didn't know that being a bad cook would cause someone to cry. Then again, those pancakes were pretty bad. She might have lost a tooth with how tough they were—just what she didn't need after a stressful night.

I walked around the island, hesitated briefly, then patted her back. "Are you alright? I didn't know they would be like that."

She sat up and looked at me. She was laughing—a tears-streaming-down-her-face, shoulders-shaking, silent laugh.

"Okay, they weren't that bad."

She nodded her head and kept laughing. "I thought I was going to be eating that pancake for the rest of my life."

That was it. She was getting hysterical, and she was making me want to laugh with her.

She took a sip of coffee. "Thanks for this. I needed something to laugh at. Besides, you make great coffee and bacon."

"I should have probably thrown out the pancake mix. It's been around a little while," I admitted with a smile. It was good to see her relaxed.

"Sorry about last night," she said.

"What happened last night?"

"I didn't mean to steal your bed. I don't remember moving from the couch."

"The couch must have been uncomfortable." I grabbed some more bacon off the plate.

"Wow. I didn't think I ever sleepwalked."

"Well, now we know." I smiled. "We'd better get those chains on your doors as soon as possible then."

Her face fell, and I could have kicked myself. She must have forgotten *why* she was sitting in my kitchen. I wished I hadn't made even a remote mention of danger. It brought back the very real problem of a burglarized house. Her relaxed posture disappeared.

"Thank you. For last night. I didn't want to stay home by myself, but today I'll get everything cleaned up, and it'll be back to normal." She smiled, but it was weak.

"Come on, we'll go over there and get whatever you need, and then we're going out for the day."

"What do you mean we're going out? It's my day off, I have to get the house cleaned up."

"It will be taken care of. Now, come on. Put on some of those stretchy, comfy pants women like to wear."

"You mean yoga pants?" She smiled.

"Whatever. Grab some tennis shoes. Wear something comfortable. We've got some errands to run."

I walked into the living room, grabbed her phone off the table, and handed it to her.

"I met your parents last night on FaceTime. They wanted you to give them a call sometime today. I told them about the break-in."

Her eyes scanned my face for a minute before she took the phone from my hand. "You must have made quite the impression if they aren't already here."

I shrugged. "They're leaving for their trip this morning."

She threw her hands in the air. "Oh great, they don't care if their oldest daughter gets murdered as long as they don't miss their anniversary trip."

I snorted. "I promised them you'd be safe with me until they catch the person who broke in."

She opened her mouth to protest, but I pressed my hand to her back and began pushing her toward the front door. She grumbled at me but slipped on her shoes.

We crossed the street, and I made her wait on the porch while I ran through the house to make sure no one was there.

It was empty.

"You can come in," I told her as I swung open the front door.

She rolled her eyes at me, but it didn't hide her smile as she said, "Thanks for permission to go into my own home."

I waited at the entryway until she disappeared into her bathroom before I started snooping around.

I opened cupboards in her kitchen, looking for something—anything—that could make me end this strange infatuation I had. She was too cute, too nice, too fun to be around. People weren't like that.

Her cupboards were full of food, and it wasn't all pre-made food. It was real ingredients. She must have cooked all the time. I snatched a handful of chocolate chips before I closed her baking cupboard.

It had been a while since I'd had good, homemade food. Mom and Dad had been asking me to come to family dinners. It'd been too long. I was even ready for Mom's chicken noodle soup that everyone hated but pretended to love just to make her happy.

Oh well, I didn't want to sit through a dinner that Brooke would have, no doubt, wrangled an invitation to.

I'd rather think of ways to distract Kylie from the break-in. Our war had been fun. Entertaining. All-consuming. When she barged into my house last night, it was all I could do to keep from grabbing her and kissing her right then and there. That would have really set her off.

Once I realized what had happened, I wanted to scoop her up into my arms and never let her go.

She had stayed in her house with a baseball bat while the intruder was still there. What had she been thinking? I had never considered myself an overprotective guy, but I wanted her to make wise decisions—like, maybe not confronting a mugger by herself with a baseball bat. I'd never felt this protective toward someone else—not even Brooke.

I grabbed the garbage can from beneath the sink and picked up shards of pottery off the living room carpet. Kylie didn't need to walk into this house with reminders that it'd been violated. I picked up a piece of pottery that had "Landon" written on it with a marker. There was dirt scattered across the living room floor, along with pieces of a cactus plant.

"Okay, I'm ready."

I stood up and looked at her. She was wearing a pink... something. It was like a dress, but it had pants. "What is that?"

She rolled her eyes at me. "It's called a jumpsuit. Where have you been living? Under a rock?"

I smirked. "Same place you've been living, Neil Armstrong."

She smacked my arm as she walked by me and out the door, but she wasn't quick enough to hide her smile.

It was going to be a fun day.

Chapter Fifteen

KYLIE

*R*ubbing my hands against the leather seat, I sat in Hagen's truck for the second time in a week. Being around him made me feel safe. Whenever I thought about staying at my house alone, I kept dreaming up worst-case scenarios. I wondered what they would title the film of my short-lived life:

Taken: From My Bathroom
The Silence of the Suburbs
The Shining of the Marketer
Louisiana Chainsaw Massacre

I would have lost my mind if I'd had to spend the night in my house by myself. Hagen managed to move his status from "pesky neighbor" up to "knight in shining armor" in a few short hours.

I thought it would have been strange to wake up in his house this morning. Though I was confused when I woke up in his bed, I felt rested and safe. It felt right, sitting there talking with Hagen over bacon and terrible pancakes.

My favorite part of the morning was when I quietly peeked around the corner and watched Hagen dance while he cooked breakfast. I loved how embarrassed he was when he caught me watching.

Even though I nearly lost a tooth when I tried those pancakes, I didn't want to be rude. It was one thing to have a prank war and give him a bloody nose, but it was something else to insult his cooking. My mom always had the rule that if you complained about the food she cooked, then you could take over the cooking chore. It didn't take me long to learn that lesson as a kid.

Ironically, now I really enjoyed cooking, but the moral of that lesson was that cooking took work, and it was impolite to insult the food someone had worked hard to prepare for you.

Hagen pulled off of the highway to a small coffee shop. He smiled at me, and I gaped. He'd smiled before—his devious smile that made me look both ways and up and down when opening any door—but this smile was a genuine, happy-to-be-here smile.

It hurt to look at. It looked so good.

He pulled up to the coffee shop window and shut off the truck. The truck was a little taller than the window, and he leaned down to order a coffee from the barista.

A couple minutes later, we each had a coffee, and Hagen was pulling back onto the road. He reached over to try and steal the chocolate-covered coffee beans that sat on top of my cup. I slapped his hand away and shoveled them into my mouth.

He chuckled.

"Why the truck?"

"Hmm?" He took another sip of coffee.

"Why do you drive a truck?"

"So that someone asks me to help them move the minute they find out."

I looked out the window so he wouldn't see me smile. "Moving seems like a nice hobby."

"You think I'm joking. I swear, people find out you drive a truck, and all of a sudden, they have a million favors to ask. They want the benefits of a truck, but then they want to lecture me on how terrible it is for the environment."

The hot coffee scalded my tongue before I answered him. "Well, you'd fit in just fine in my family. It's like a rite of passage to own a truck in the Boone family. Of course, we're a bunch of blue collar workers and uneducated rednecks, if you ask anyone else," I told him with a wink.

"You don't drive a truck. Does that mean they kicked you out of the family?"

I debated how to answer that one. "Big trucks and I don't get along?"

"Is that a question?"

"No?" I asked.

He laughed. "I bet there's a good story to this."

At least if I told him the humiliating truth, I'd give him a good reason to keep laughing and smiling, and that was something I wanted. "Every time I drive a truck, I hit something: lightposts, mailboxes, other cars, anything that can be bumped into. I don't know why. I'm an excellent driver, usually."

He raised his eyebrows but kept his eyes on the road.

"Don't judge me—you've never ridden with me."

"It sounds like I never should."

"Pfft, you'd be so safe you'd be bored out of your mind. Besides, I have amazing reflexes. I can hit the brakes faster than anyone else I've ridden with."

Hagen pulled into the parking lot of the hardware store and parked. He turned to me. "I hate riding with other people.

So much that I'll drive myself even if I'm meeting friends a couple hours away. Then, you just told me you hit all kinds of things. You'd have to drug me to get me in the car with you."

He looked so serious it made me almost want to do it. "Okay. Let's make a bet. If I win the bet, you have to ride with me somewhere. If you win—well, I don't know—I guess I won't make you ride with me anywhere."

He tapped a finger against the steering wheel. "If I win, you have to bake me some muffins and cookies."

"What if they turn out like your pancakes did?"

He smiled. "I've tasted your cooking before. It was really good."

I studied him. I had never baked him anything, and I distinctly remembered bringing home my cookies that I tried to give him the first day I met him.

Then, I remembered that he had been in my house when he planted the snake in my bathtub. I had made cupcakes for Susan's birthday. I thought I had been short a few cupcakes, but I figured it was all in my head.

I rested my elbow on the console and leaned toward him. "How many did you eat?"

Hagen leaned an elbow on the console, his arm brushing mine as he leaned close. "Five. They were amazing."

He didn't even try to deny it. I wasn't sure if I should have been outraged or pleased that he thought they were delicious.

"So, what's the bet going to be?" he prompted.

I hadn't thought that far ahead. I wanted him to have to ride in the car with me, but I didn't know how to go about it. "I'll have to think on it."

"Fine by me. Now, come on, we'll find some strong chain locks for your doors."

He jumped out of the truck and raced around to my

side to open the door for me. I hadn't expected him to be such a gentleman—or maybe I did.

He was destroying my preconceived ideas of him being a villain. It was hard to stay mad at someone who protected you, fed you bacon, and bought you coffee.

He held my hand as I climbed out of the truck. I was going to have to try and tuck my heart back into my chest if I wasn't careful. I needed to find a fault of his to dwell on for a while.

It didn't take long to find that fault. Turns out, he was horrible to shop with. Horrible. It was like shopping with my mother.

He asked the hardware store employees at least five hundred questions about chain locks while we were in the hardware store. I had enough time to organize my five thousand recipes I'd saved on Pinterest.

Tapping his muscled arm with my granola bar—thank goodness I always packed snacks—I turned his attention to me. "Hagen, I appreciate how thorough you are, but I'm sure if we just get one of these strong-looking locks, it will be fine."

He shook his head. "I'm going to make sure this chain will hold for you."

"You know what would make me feel safe? If you cooked up some more pancakes and let me use them like throwing stars."

His lips twitched, and I knew I was on the right track. He was taking this shopping thing a little too seriously.

"If I put a sign on my house that says "Protected by Hagen's Pancakes," no one would even dream of trying to break in."

He chuckled. The harried employee that Hagen had been badgering rushed over with a set of locks. "These are them. These are the strongest and are highly recommended by a local policeman who has them in his house."

"But what about—"

"These will work perfect. Thank you," I cut Hagen off.

I smiled at the employee, and his shoulders sagged with relief when I took the locks from him.

"Come on, Hagen, there's a sale at the home store. You need some decor in your house, and I'm just the person to help you with that."

He turned around as though he were going to head farther back in the store, but I grabbed his hand. "Oh no, you've harassed these good people enough for one day. We're paying and leaving."

With a sigh, he turned and followed me up to the counter.

He didn't let go of my hand, and I didn't want him to.

Chapter Sixteen

KYLIE

*W*ednesday morning, I sat down at my desk and began setting up my things for the day. Hagen insisted on driving me to work today. He told me he was concerned about me hitting lampposts and mailboxes on the way. I didn't protest this because it was an excuse to spend more time with him. We'd settled into a nice routine as roommates, and he'd even let me decorate his living room for him. It was strangely domestic and natural to do it. He complained about having to hold up so many frames while I decided where they should go. He didn't think I noticed him smiling while he did it.

Today was the day I met with our new client, the owner of the gym.

I finished turning on my computer and began sorting through the mail that sat on my desk. Trey was in charge of distributing everyone's mail first thing in the morning. The mail that sat on my desk was probably accumulated from the weekend.

There was a letter from a client, Hyacinth Perdue, thanking me for the work I had done for her store. She owned a quilt and craft shop downtown where she taught classes in the evening. She was, hands down, my favorite client I'd ever worked with. I grabbed a sticky note and wrote down a reminder to sign up for her summer beading class before I opened her letter. In the letter, she thanked me again for helping advertise her store. She informed me that she was starting a second quilting class because the first one had gotten so full. She also invited me over for tea —something I planned to take her up on. Maybe if I got off work early enough tomorrow, I'd stop by the store and say hello.

There was a large, manila envelope at the bottom of the mail stack. I opened it and pulled out the contents.

A picture. It was a picture of me.

Actually, it was a picture of Hagen and me. We were sitting in the cab of his truck. The camera had been zoomed in enough that I couldn't see where we were parked—or if we were parked.

Before I had time to grab my phone and call that nice detective, Rick, Trey knocked on my open doorway.

"Mrs. Vandenmeyer wanted me to tell you that the new client is here. She wants you to come to her office right away."

"Thanks, Trey. I'll be right there."

Dropping the envelope and picture on my desk, I gathered up my tablet and coffee cup, then headed to Susan's office.

The door was closed, so I tucked the tablet under my arm so I could knock.

I heard Susan call for me to come in. I fumbled with the doorknob, trying to not drop the tablet or, even more importantly, my coffee. Once I was qualified as a professional juggler, I opened the door and stepped inside.

Susan sat on the cream-colored couch with her hand

resting on the knee of a man who sat next to her. The man had his head bent over his phone with an arm slung around Susan's shoulders.

Well, it was definitely the most awkward meeting I'd ever walked into. Normally, Susan sat behind her desk, and the client sat in the uncomfortable chairs. The couch was purely for aesthetic purposes; no one actually sat on it. I didn't even know it could hold the weight of an adult. And why was Susan touching him? What kind of an account did she land?

The man finished typing on his phone then looked up and smiled at me.

"Jason?"

Jason—from the gym—stood from the couch. "Kylie, how are you?"

He walked over and gave me a hug. I tried to hug him back with my T-rex arms, but it was hard to hug when your arms were full.

"What are you doing here?"

He released me and pulled me over to sit on the couch with them. Jason sat in the middle. I'd never known he was such a cozy soul. In fact, I didn't know that Susan was that way, either. Yet, there she sat, leaning against him. I tried to lean farther into the arm of the couch, but Jason was not a small guy, and I bumped against him every time I shifted.

He turned to me and smiled. "I'm your new client. I'm expanding the gym."

Susan leaned forward to look around Jason's sizable chest so that she could talk to me. "This is why I wanted you to personally handle this account. I wanted to make sure he had the most creative mind working on it."

Then, she reached up and patted his cheek like he was five years old.

I was so distracted that I came up with a brilliant reply. "Okay."

"So, now we can get down to the details," Susan said. "Why don't you show us what you have?"

I rested the tablet on my lap and took a giant gulp of coffee. I should have added a shot of something else today. "Since I didn't know what kind of gym we were talking about, I focused on thinking about the thing that holds people back from going to the gym."

"They can't afford it? Laziness?" Jason asked.

"No, it's fear."

"Fear?"

"People are scared they won't belong. Some people are intimidated by all the equipment. Everybody wants to feel like they have somewhere to fit in. Gyms are usually marketed toward people who are already fit and in the prime of their life. If you want to widen your customer base, you're going to have to show them how easy it is to go to the gym."

"I take it you have experience with this?"

"Yes! I'm admittedly a gym coward. The only reason I started going to your gym was because I didn't want to get kidnapped and killed. Now that I know it's your gym we're talking about, I think this idea would be perfect. When I first showed up at the gym, you took the time to make sure I didn't kill myself when I tried the elliptical. You showed me the weight machines—maybe someday I'll actually use them. I watched you help an elderly woman onto the treadmill just the other day. You're good at making people feel like they could fit in at your gym; you just have to let the rest of the world know it."

"All right."

"All right?"

"Yeah, I think you have a good point. What are your ideas?"

"If possible, it'd be great to do a video of some of your clients, or of you teaching them how to use different machines. If you have a beginner's yoga class, or something like that, that's also a great way to get people in there, because they'll feel like they fit in with a bunch of other beginners. We can market your gym as the people's gym."

"Sounds good. What do you think, Mom?"

Susan studied the tablet. "It's an angle that isn't explored as much as it should be."

I nodded in agreement, and then Jason's words sunk in. "Mom? You're his mother? How did I not know this?"

Both Susan and Jason laughed—they had the same exact laugh. They had the same mouth. Jason must have gotten his height from his father, though, because he had several inches on Susan.

"I don't usually have time during the day to stop by the office. Mom and I meet for lunch somewhere closer to the gym," Jason explained.

"I'd heard from Jason that you went to his gym, so we thought you would be the perfect one to run the campaign for him. You have first-hand knowledge of the gym and how it functions. I told Jason that you would be just perfect for this."

"Well, thank you, Susan. It's nice to know I'm doing a good job. I am just so surprised that you're his mother."

"Didn't think I had it in me, did you?"

Kylie, don't insert your foot in your mouth, I told myself. "You just seem so young. It's hard to imagine you having a grown child."

"Nice save," Jason whispered to me when Susan stood to refill her coffee cup.

"I thought so," I muttered. Usually, I didn't let my thoughts jump out like that, but I had been so surprised to find out that Jason was Susan's son. "You know, I thought we were friends now. Friends don't let friends walk into giant surprises."

Jason chuckled, and Susan came back to sit on the couch with a fresh cup of coffee. The rest of the morning, we sat cozied up on the couch, discussing marketing ideas and Jason's overall vision for his gym.

It was the perfect distraction from obsessing over Hagen. I'd even forgotten about the pictures I'd received in the mail.

———

My parents were planning to adopt Hagen. It was the most reasonable explanation. They couldn't stop singing his praises. They must have been having an early midlife crisis and were wanting another child—because four wasn't enough.

I called and talked to Dad on the way home after work, and he informed me he had help on the way. I had a pretty good idea what that meant, and I wasn't sure how crazy I was about the idea.

He asked after Hagen and all about his job, friends, philosophy of life, etcetera. My mom jumped on the line to tell me she texted Hagen a picture of their hotel and thanked him for watching me, because if it hadn't been for him, they wouldn't have felt comfortable leaving me. I felt like I was about ten years old and left with the babysitter.

I had to admit that they had a point, though. Hagen was being exceptionally sweet and made me feel safe. Besides the whoopee cushion on my bar stool—well, technically, it was his barstool, but I'd claimed it since I'd been staying there—he hadn't done anything drastic. Just small pranks.

I may have short-sheeted his guest bed last night. He had definitely put that rubber snake on the king bed where I was sleeping. Two days ago, I stuffed just enough toilet paper into the ends of his running shoes to make them uncomfortable. I wasn't sure he'd even figured that one out yet, because as he drove me to work, he mentioned he needed to buy some shoes and might be a little late picking me up from work. I told him I'd get a ride home with someone else, and he passed me a spare key to his house.

On my lunch break, after a long morning meeting with Jason and Susan the Mother, I had a copy of Hagen's key made—in case of an emergency. I didn't know how everything from this week was going to affect our little war, but I was going to be prepared for whatever may come.

I stepped through my front door and hurriedly shut off the alarm Hagen had paid to install in my house. I wasn't sure how I felt about that. He didn't make a big deal about it. I think his exact words were, "It's done." I couldn't believe how fast he'd gotten a company out to install it.

When I told him I wanted to pay him back, he told me, "Too bad."

That was why I was risking being in my house by myself. I knew he liked baked goodies, and I wanted to do something nice for him for a change. I grabbed a tote bag from my front closet and began scooping all the various ingredients I would need into the bag. I grabbed a couple muffin tins and cookie sheets from the cupboard next to my oven then reset the alarm and headed across the street.

I still didn't feel comfortable enough to be at my house by myself, especially after the pictures this morning. Those notes were personal. I should have told Hagen about them, but I didn't want him to think I was jumping to some crazy conclusions.

After lining up the ingredients on Hagen's kitchen island. I preheated the oven and looked around for a mixing bowl. The closest thing I found was a giant, plastic bowl. It would have to do. I spent the next hour making banana and lemon-poppy-seed muffins. It felt wonderful. Whenever I baked, I shut off my mind. I thought about inconsequential things, like will it rain this weekend? And just how many chocolate chips are too many? Correct answer: there are never enough.

When I pulled the muffins out of the oven, I filled a plate to take over to Dave. I'd been meaning to do something nice for him since he had always let me borrow tools whenever I needed them. After seeing the stash of tools in Hagen's garage, I thought I might have found a new lender.

Every drawer, box, and reused coffee can was clearly labeled. He probably counted his bolts before he went to bed at night. Knowing that a tool was being borrowed would probably drive him insane. I'd have to remember that for later.

I had just finished washing the dishes when I heard the front door open.

"Honey, I'm home!"

My heart dropped into my stomach at Hagen's voice. My cheeks flushed, and I hurriedly dried the muffin tin before I set it down on the counter. He might have been joking, but my heart seemed to think it was real, because it wasn't letting me catch my breath. My mind flashed forward ten years to picture Hagen and me chasing a couple of cute kids around the house. I shook my head to get rid of the image.

Hagen walked into the kitchen with a smirk on his face.

He set his running shoes on my barstool—yes, I'd claimed it since I'd been staying at his house.

"I decided to take my old running shoes back to the store since I only bought them a month ago. They've been hurting my feet. Imagine my surprise when the shoe clerk found toilet paper stuffed in the ends." He stalked around the island toward me.

Instead of running for my life, I laughed uncontrollably as I pictured his embarrassment at realizing his mistake. "Did you tell them you were trying to fit into your big brother's shoes?"

"That's it." Hagen leapt for me and latched onto my elbow before I could make a getaway. He reeled me in until I was touching his chest. "You've got it coming."

Wildly reaching for the only defense available, I managed to grab it and waved it slowly beneath his nose.

He closed his eyes and sniffed. "That smells amazing. Where did you buy those?"

I grinned as he released me and grabbed the muffin out of my hand. "I made them."

He opened his eyes and looked at me in wonder. It was as if I had told him I invented electricity.

He peeled the muffin liner off and ate half the muffin in one bite. I bit my lip as I waited for the verdict. I didn't know why, but I really wanted him to like them.

It had nothing to do with my daydream of mini Hagens and Kylies running around. Nothing at all.

Instead of saying anything, he shoved the rest of the muffin in his mouth and grabbed another one off the counter. I'd never seen anyone's lack of manners look as good as Hagen's. In fact, it nearly melted my heart. There was no better compliment to a cook or baker than to see someone eat their food with abandon.

If someone said they liked your food, they might have

been fibbing. If someone inhaled three—no, four—muffins in a row, it showed they actually did like them.

He swallowed the last bite of muffin then looked at me. "I'm never letting you leave if you're going to make things like this all the time."

A lot of people took my cooking and baking skills for granted. I loved to do it, so I always offered to bring something to dinners, family get-togethers, etcetera. My family had gotten used to me making all sorts of delicious things, so it felt good that someone new was appreciating those skills.

"Am I forgiven about the shoes?"

"What shoes?" He smiled, and my world tilted sideways.

If he smiled like that all the time, I would make him muffins for breakfast, lunch, and dinner. I cleared my throat and hopefully caught the drool before it escaped. He was joking around, and I was forgetting that he wasn't the guy who I was going to spend the rest of my life with.

What if hanging out with Hagen caused me to be distracted and not realize when true love crossed my path?

Yes, I was attracted to Hagen, but I wanted the full nine yards: love, marriage, and the baby carriage. He wasn't even looking for a girlfriend. He was a nice guy, making sure his neighbor didn't get murdered.

Hagen headed out of the kitchen and tossed his shoes inside his bedroom door. No wonder his room was a disaster zone.

"I'm going to run a plate of these over to Dave."

Hagen turned around, a crestfallen look on his face. "You mean they're not all for us?"

"No, not all forty-eight of them," I laughed.

He grumbled under his breath, snagged a plate full of muffins off the counter, then headed toward the bathroom.

"Um, are you showering with those muffins?"

"Haters gonna hate!" he hollered.

Hagen was so different from the man I'd first met. Maybe I'd caught him on a bad day when I came over to introduce myself. Maybe his grandma had died that day. But other than sparking an all out war between us, I had yet to see that version of Hagen again. He was everything a man should have been. He was goofy when it was just us. It made me wonder if I was the only one he acted silly with, but I guessed I'd never know.

Chapter Seventeen

HAGEN

*W*hen I stepped out of the shower, Kylie was already back from taking the muffins to Dave. There were still two plates full of muffins on the counter, thank goodness. That girl could cook, and I was so glad she'd made enough for me. I didn't feel like sharing with anyone else. I didn't care if Dave had loaned her his firstborn child instead of tools; I still didn't want to share those muffins.

My phone chimed on the counter where I had left it when I got back from the store. I couldn't believe I had let her get away with stuffing my tennis shoes. I'd been intent on revenge until she waved that muffin in my face. Her cooking skills were like a weapon, a tactical move to keep me from retaliating. It was brilliant, and it worked. I was pretty sure I'd let her get away with anything if she fed me delicious muffins all the time.

"What are we watching tonight?" I asked as I sat down on the couch next to Kylie. She had officially taken over my favorite spot on the couch. It was a travesty.

She glanced at me with a little smile and stretched out

her feet to rest them on the coffee table. Her yellow painted toes poked out from the bottom of her yoga pants. "Home renovation shows. I need to get inspired for my backyard. I've started on it, but I'd like to finish landscaping. Maybe build a pergola or something."

"Who are you going to hire to do it?"

"I think I'll try and do it myself. How hard could it be?"

I stared at her. "Have you ever built something like that before?"

She folded her arms across her chest and glared at me. "Do you think I can't do it because I'm a woman?"

"No, I think you can't do it because I didn't see a single tool in your garage. My guess is you've never needed to use those types of tools before." I reached over and flicked an imaginary chip off her shoulder.

She sighed. "Fair enough. No, I'm actually terrible at building things. I tried to build a birdhouse this year. I thought it would look nice in the backyard, so I borrowed a hammer from Dave."

"How'd that turn out?"

She frowned. "I roasted some nice marshmallows over that wood."

"Well, let's find you a plan that looks like what you want, and I'll help you build it."

She looked at me in surprise. "You will?"

I shrugged. "Of course."

"Thank you!" She leaned forward and, for one second, I thought she was going to hug me—or even better, kiss me—but she reached past me for the remote that sat on the arm of the couch. "Let's get inspired."

An hour later and I was ready to tear my eyes out. I didn't know renovation shows could be so dramatic. Heaven forbid that the paint color was too eggshell and not enough cream. Really? This was a thing? No wonder Kylie was concerned about my undecorated house.

I glanced over at her, and to my surprise, she wasn't watching the show. In fact, she seemed to be staring at the wall, completely zoned out.

"You okay?"

She jumped and smacked her foot against the coffee table. "Don't scare me like that!"

Her cheeks were white, and her eyes were wide.

"Something's wrong, isn't it?"

She fidgeted with her hands a minute before she leaned over and hit the mute button on the TV. "I have to show you something."

She stood up and went to grab her purse from the entryway. She set it down on the coffee table in front of me. "I've been getting these notes. Even though I didn't think they meant anything, I mentioned them to the police after the break-in. They said I was probably worried over nothing. I tried to believe them, but then, today, I got this."

She reached into her purse then let out a blood-curdling scream as she pulled out the robotic spider I had slipped in there when I first got home. I couldn't stop myself from laughing. She dropped it on the table where it landed on its back, the legs moving quickly in the air. She turned and glared at me. It was the only warning I had before she leapt into my lap and began swinging at me. I couldn't even protect myself since I was too busy laughing. She caught me on the side of the head, my chest, my arms, my thigh—that one was a little too close.

Grasping her wrists, I pinned them to my chest. "I'm sorry." I tried to sound sincere, but there was still a trace of laughter in my voice.

She managed to wriggle her fingers free and pinch me. "You don't sound sorry. I was already on edge when I was grabbing my purse, and then I found that–that thing in there!"

"It was just a little harmless payback for the shoes. Don't be mad."

"Well, I'm mad!"

I ran my hand up and down her back. She seemed so small sitting on my lap. I could have easily held her to me with one arm. I splayed my hand against her lower back, and it reached from side to side.

She started to melt against me when I reached my second hand to the back of her neck and began to knead the muscles there. I was complicating things. This was turning into more than friends.

I swallowed as I realized I wanted that for us. I wanted some type of future. When I came home from work and found her with a big, mischievous grin on her face over the prank she'd played, I knew I wanted to spend my life with someone like that. With her. Someone who could laugh easily, who didn't mind my immature sense of humor, or my terrible dance moves.

But right then, I needed to find out what was worrying her so much.

"Tell me."

"Only if you promise no more fake spiders—or snakes."

I nodded. "No more fake spiders or snakes."

"Good."

"Only real ones."

She sat up and pressed her forehead against mine while she wrapped her hands around my neck as if she was going to choke me. I could smell the sweet muffins on her breath, and I could see the different shades of brown in her eyes. "If you ever, and I mean ever, put a real snake or spider anywhere near me, it will be the last thing you do."

I had to admit, it was charming when she threatened my life like that. But it was hard to take her seriously when she couldn't even wrap her hands around my neck. What was she going to do, hug me to death?

"Noted."

She leaned back and released my neck. She pushed out of my arms and sat beside me on the couch as she riffled through her purse again. I immediately missed having her in my arms. I began wondering how I could arrange having her there again.

"Look at this, and tell me what you think."

She handed me a large envelope. I opened it and pulled a piece of paper out. It was a picture of Kylie and me in the cab of my truck.

"What is this?"

"I don't know. You tell me. Who would be taking pictures of us?"

I studied the picture. It was grainy, as though someone had used a low-quality camera then zoomed in. Neither Kylie nor I were looking directly at the camera.

I looked at the return address on the envelope.

"It's the address of a Piggly Wiggly in town. It's the same address they used on the other envelopes."

"*Other* envelopes? What do you mean?"

She sat close enough that our arms were touching as she explained. "There were these notes. I didn't think anything of it at first. Actually, I thought it was a bad marketing technique or something, but then they started to get personal, and then there was the break-in with nothing taken. Maybe I'm being paranoid, I don't know. But this picture was in my mail at the office today."

"Here," Kylie said as she handed me a few more papers from her purse. I unfolded them and read the notes.

. . .

Kylie,

You might not realize it yet, but you are the one for me.
We'll be each other's forever. We'll be the ones who last.
Signed,
The One Who Loves You.

The second one:

You are everything to me.

"One was sent to my house, and one was sent to my office at work. The picture came to the office today, too."

"And you told this to the police?"

"They didn't think there was anything connecting the notes with the break-in. They said to let them know if anything more showed up."

The police had told us that the recent break-ins in the area had all reported stolen prescription drugs. It would have made sense that nothing was missing if all they were looking for was prescription drugs. Or that could have been explained away if the break-in was because of a stalker and not a thief. "Did you tell them about the picture from today?"

She grimaced. "Not yet."

"Kylie! You should have called them right away! What if this creep had been waiting for you after work? Why didn't you call me?"

"Okay, Dad," she said, and then she rolled her eyes. She actually rolled her eyes at me. It was like I had a toddler living in my house.

I stood up and stomped over to my phone on the

counter. I ignored the text message that was waiting for me. I really needed to block Brooke's number.

I called Rick and put him on speakerphone.

"What's going on?" he answered.

"Kylie has a stalker."

"We don't know—" I gently clamped my hand over her mouth to stop her protest.

"He's been sending her notes, and today, he sent her a picture of us in the cab of my truck."

"What exactly were you doing in the cab of your truck?" Rick asked with a chuckle.

"Driving," I snapped. "Now, any chance the break-in is related to this, and what do we do?"

"Well, there's no way to put out a restraining order without knowing who it is. To be perfectly honest, there really isn't anything we can do until there's contact. I'm assuming that was Kylie I heard there with you?"

Something sharp cut the palm of my hand. Her teeth. She shoved my arm away and leaned closer to the phone. "Hi, Rick, it's Kylie here."

"Hey, Kylie. You know, that's some serious business if people are sending you pictures and notes. You can't be too careful with that kind of stuff. I wish I could help, but until you have a name for us, there's not much we can do. Did he mail the notes?"

"Yes, but it was the address of a Piggly Wiggly in town."

"Did you happen to notice the date stamped on the stamps?"

"Um, no. Let me look really quick." She flipped over the envelopes while I watched over her shoulder.

"There's no stamp on them."

It was silent on the other end for a few seconds. "Kylie, do you have an alarm on your house?"

"Yes, Hagen had someone install it this weekend."

"Good. Arm it every time you enter or leave your house. Have Hagen give you my personal number. Hagen, I need to talk to you a minute."

I glanced at Kylie before I took the phone off speaker-phone. I headed into the kitchen and grabbed a muffin before I stepped out onto my back deck.

"What is it, Rick?"

"Look, we all realize how much you like this girl, so this shouldn't be a chore for you, but keep an eye on her. Whoever is sending her these things is obviously close to her. Dropping something off in her work mailbox and getting that picture of the two of you? I didn't want to scare her, especially since the chief wouldn't even bother to look into a case like this, but I'd guess you have someone with a full-fledged obsession. Can you walk her to and from her car in the evenings? Maybe check in on her at her house, make sure she's fine? Even with an alarm, she's vulnerable. Usually, stalkers are someone you've met before. She could open the door to whoever it is."

I stretched my legs out when I sat down on my lawn chair. I debated whether or not I should tell him that Kylie was staying with me. He would tell Kara, and then she would tell Linley. And Linley, the self-proclaimed love doctor, would never get off my case again. Darn that sister-in-law.

"She's uh…well, she's been staying here with me."

Rick chuckled. "So that's the way it is."

"No, no. Don't read into this. I wanted her to feel safe. And now she's stolen my king-size bed and decorated my living room."

"Oh, this is good. I can't wait to tell Kara so she can tell Linley."

"That's what I was afraid of."

"They have been dying for you to date someone they liked. When that girl walked into your house, swinging her baseball bat at you, we all fell in love a little. Ask her out."

"You know I can't do that." I sighed.

"No, actually, I don't know that. I don't know what's wrong with you, man. You're a great guy. I'm pretty sure a crazy number of women would be overjoyed to be with you. You're the only one who doesn't think you're good enough to be happy with someone."

"Yeah, well, Brooke said—"

"Screw what Brooke said."

"My mom agreed with her."

"No offense, man, but your mom might not win any motherly awards. Besides, I'm glad you broke up with Brooke. Think about how much happier you are now."

Rick wasn't wrong—unfortunately. I only wished I had recognized the truth sooner, before Brooke had managed to get inside my head and plant a giant seed—no, a tree— of doubt in my mind. That seed had sprung into a full-blown redwood by the time I realized her poisonous nature.

"I'll think about it. But right now, let's focus on keeping her safe."

"Sounds good. If she has any more contact, or anything that could help us, have her call me or the station. We might be able to open a case if we have enough to go on."

"Thanks, man. Say hi to Kara and the baby for me."

"Will do."

Rick hung up the phone, and I headed back inside. Kylie was curled up on the couch, eating ice cream out of the carton, watching reality TV.

"Stressed?"

She nodded and passed me a spoon. "I'll share."

I leaned over the ice cream carton and scooped a giant bite of the chocolate into my mouth and turned to watch the TV.

"What is wrong with that woman's lips?"

Kylie licked a little bit of chocolate off of her lips. "They're called lip implants."

"That's just not natural."

Kylie chuckled. "I think that's the point."

"What if men started getting lip work done?" I stuck my lips out how I imagined they would look.

She snort-laughed. "Stop! Please stop. I can't breathe. You look like a platypus."

I grinned. It felt nice to just be *me* around someone. I hated letting people see me at my goofiest. But with Kylie, it just came naturally.

I reached over and squeezed her hand. "You're going to be okay."

I wasn't sure she heard me through her laughter.

Chapter Eighteen

KYLIE

"Yo! Anybody seen crazy Kylie?" a voice yelled from inside my house.

I slammed the dryer lid closed and turned it on. After work, I had gone home to do some housekeeping to prep for my new guests. It would be the first night I spent in my house since the break-in. Bless Kara's heart, because she had sent someone over to clean my house for me the day Hagen and I had been out buying locks.

It was time for me to move back into my own house.

I was getting too comfortable at Hagen's. It felt too domestic and homey, which, ironically, was exactly what I wanted, but I'd rather have it be with someone who was in love with me, not a neighbor who was just as likely to kill me as love me.

Walking into the living room, I found my cousin Page standing in the entryway with a large bag.

"I heard you could use some company," she said. She dropped the bag, and we hugged. "Uncle Todd called me."

"Of course he did," I laughed. My dad would pack me up and move me home if he could. He might not have wanted to miss out on his anniversary trip, but he would still make sure I was safe. He sent a protective detail in the form of my cousin. He made a wise choice sending Page. She had the best swing when we played bayou baseball.

"He's sending everyone, just so you know. Jenny, Jordan, Mack."

I snorted. Apparently, Dad thought he needed to send the whole family. Our other cousins knew how to have a good time, and they would be a welcome distraction from the creep who broke into my house.

"Oh, good grief, no. I want my house to be standing when this is all over."

"I know, that's what I told your dad, but he didn't think there was such a thing as too many cousins. I think there is." She grimaced, and I couldn't help but agree with her reaction.

We might as well book a room at the hospital, because we were going to need it. My cousins' antics reached new levels when they all got together. It was like getting three toddlers together and letting them drink a case of energy drinks. Page would deny any involvement, but I knew that she often gave them some of their "best" ideas.

"They can't stay in my house. They'll burn it down."

"You've got that right." She walked into the kitchen and pulled a lemonade from the fridge. "Now, why was your good-looking neighbor glaring at me when I pulled in your driveway?"

My heart stuttered for reasons I didn't care to think about as I replied, "He may or may not have promised to keep an eye on things ever since the break-in. He was probably making sure you weren't stopping by to murder me."

A loud knock sounded on the door. I shrieked. Page made a gurgling noise. I finally summoned up enough courage to walk over to the door and look through the peephole.

"Speak of the devil," I said as I swung the door open. Hagen stood on my porch, hands on his hips. "What's up?"

He looked annoyed about something. I wasn't sure why he would have been mad. I hadn't done anything to him in a while. I was starting to turn into dream neighbor material. Maybe he had found my missing sock in his couch cushions. Socks do stink after a while.

"You had a hide-a-key on your front porch." He said it in a low voice as he leaned his head down so we were looking in each other's eyes.

"Yes, it's a new practice for forgetful people who lose their keys. How did you know?"

"The girl who just got here knew exactly where it was."

"That's because she's my cousin. All Boones hide their keys in the same place—makes it easy for visiting relatives."

His cheeks flushed, and the vein in his neck protruded. "Are you insane?"

"She's never been formally diagnosed," Page informed him from behind me.

He glanced over my head at Page. "Who are you?"

"The cousin—and temporary bodyguard until the psycho is caught. My name's Page," she answered as she reached around me to shake Hagen's hand. Hagen smiled his megawatt smile at Page. Why was he kind to her when he had been so rude to me the first time we met? Double standard much?

"So tell me, Page, don't you think it's a little crazy to leave a key on the porch when there's a stalker out there?"

"I couldn't agree more. Come on in, and we'll talk about Kylie like she can't hear us." Page grabbed his arm and dragged him over to the couch. "Coke?"

She began to raid the fridge like she had lived here for five years instead of five minutes.

She tossed me a can of Coke then pointed to the seat next to Hagen on the couch. Page dropped another can into Hagen's hand then curled up on the loveseat next to the couch.

I sat criss-cross applesauce on the couch next to Hagen.

"How is it being Kylie's neighbor? She said you've been making her feel safe knowing you're keeping an eye on things."

I glared at Page. What she said was true, but I didn't want Hagen to think I was going soft. I took a big drink of Coke then began to choke.

Hagen slapped a big hand on my back a couple of times then left it there while he answered Page.

"You know, Kylie threatens to shove me in her garbage can almost every time I see her," he said with a frown that didn't hide the twinkle in his eyes.

Page nodded seriously. "She has some violent tendencies. She gets it from her mother's side. The Boones are much more stable."

I snorted and rolled my eyes. Hagen tapped his fingers against my shoulder—not that I could have forgotten his hand was there.

"I take it you're a Boone too," he said to Page.

"Of course. We bring class to the family," Page said with a straight face. I always envied her ability to deadpan.

She continued, "So, has she managed to stuff you in the garbage can yet?"

Hagen smirked at me. "She tried. She did give me a bloody nose."

Page's eyes widened slightly as she looked at me. I shrugged. "He cracked my head."

"In that case, it's justified. So what are your intentions toward my cousin now that you've cracked her skull?" She folded her arms across her chest.

I wasn't sure how Page transitioned to a concerned father figure in two seconds, but the change was impressive. I half expected for her to grab a shotgun out of her duffel bag.

Hagen decided to play along, because he removed his arm from my shoulders and set his drink down. He folded his hands and rested his elbows on his knees.

"Well, first I have to convince her to stop picking on me. Then, I'm going to ask her on a date. I'll propose on Christmas Eve, and then we'll get married and have two and a half kids."

"Two and a half?"

"Maybe three. In the meantime, I plan on trying to keep her safe. Even if it means chewing her out for leaving a key out there where anyone could get it."

I swallowed the lump in my throat as he described his plan. Even though I knew he was joking, it made my heart speed up. But Hagen wasn't looking for a girlfriend, I reminded myself.

"Well, what do you bring to the relationship?"

"I have a job."

"That's always a good start," she said in a patronizing tone. "Good health insurance?"

"You guys are insane," I told them.

Page ignored me and continued, "What I want to know is what will I get out of the deal if you and Kylie were an item?"

Hagen shrugged. "Keys to my vacation home?"

Some soda came back up my nose, and Page made a strange gulping noise.

"You have a vacation home? How old are you?"

"Technically, it's my brothers' and mine, but yes, I do. Twenty-eight."

I rested my chin in my hand to keep from staring at him.

"Tell me more about this vacation home and cracking Kylie's head open," Page told him.

"Well, the house is on the beach in Florida. It's just a modest little beach cabin, so I wouldn't get your hopes up that it's a mansion. We have a cabin in Colorado, but it's pretty rustic, too."

"I don't care if it's a tent on the beach or a shack in the woods, I'm calling in a friend favor."

I flattened my lips and glared at her. "You guys aren't friends. You can't call in friend favors."

"Of course we're friends! Isn't that right, Hagen?"

Hagen looked like he was one second away from laughing, but he managed to answer her. "We'll be best friends. Maybe we could make those little bracelets for each other."

I rolled my eyes and bit my tongue to keep from laughing. They probably would make great friends. Page was fun to be around, and she was good at being friends with guys.

"Now, about trying to kill my cousin…"

"She's exaggerating. Besides, she started it."

"I certainly did not start it," I protested. "But I will finish it." I set down my coke and turned to face him full on.

Before I could have done anything, he wrapped an arm around my shoulders and tucked me close to his side. "Let's not fight in front of company, dear."

I pinched his side, but it was the only retaliation I had in me. I didn't want him to take his arm away.

Chapter Nineteen

KYLIE

riday morning, I skipped going into the office and, instead, ran a few errands then stopped by the gym. Three more of my cousins were coming to stay today. It made me feel bad that they were using up their own vacation time, but I hoped they knew I would have done the same thing for them if they needed me.

If it hadn't been for those notes I'd gotten, I wouldn't have been as creeped out by the whole break-in thing. As it was, I didn't even want to argue with my parents about having four Boone cousins in my house. It was almost worth the risk.

I was a strong, independent woman who could take care of herself—until there was a possible chance of a stalker and imminent death in my future. Then, I'd take any assistance I could get. Crazy cousins and neighbors were welcome to apply. Page slept in my twin bed with me, and I didn't even object.

I headed to the locker room to change into my shorts and tank top, glad that I ran my errands before I worked out. I entered the digital code to get into my locker and pulled it open. A piece of paper laid on the bottom of my locker. Hopefully, it wasn't a complaint from Jason about me accidentally freezing the treadmill screen the other day. I really needed to find a new gym now that he was a client of ours, but I liked this one. And I liked Jason.

I grabbed the piece of paper and opened it up.

I can see how perfect we are for each other, why can't you?

Tucked inside was a pressed flower. It was the same block printing that had been on the other notes. I dropped both of them and slammed the locker. I snatched up my bag and ran from the room.

There would be no working out today. My heart was already trying to climb into my throat. I dashed down the hallway and rounded the corner, only to slam into a chest.

I shrieked as I started to fall backwards.

Large hands wrapped around my arms.

"Whoa! I'm so sorry, Kylie. I wasn't paying attention." Jason pulled me upright again, and I stopped screaming. "I didn't mean to scare you."

"No, it's okay. I'm fine," I said. My hand shook as I brushed my hair behind my ear.

"Hey, did you find that thing I left for you?"

I glanced back toward the locker room and then back at him. It couldn't have been. We'd decided to be friends. He couldn't possibly have been the one who was sending me notes. Or could he?

He knew a lot about me: my routines, my home address, my work schedule. Jason knew all of it. It would have been easy for him to drop something in my locker or the mailbox at work.

That picture of Hagen and me could have been taken when Hagen dropped me off at the gym.

"Crazy stalker." I choked on my own tongue then darted around him, leaving him standing there looking perplexed.

————

I parked my car in my driveway and rested my face in my hands. Why did I have to freak out on Jason like that? I didn't know why I panicked. He had looked concerned when I said "crazy stalker." Then again, what if he *was* the crazy stalker? What did he even want with me? He said he'd left me something, but that note was the only thing in my locker.

Because I was preoccupied trying to figure out if Jason was my stalker, I didn't see it coming until it slammed into the side of my car.

A body was sliding down the side of my car window. I screamed as a face slid into view.

The grotesque face grinned at me.

My fear-induced scream turned into a cry of outrage. The man stepped back, away from my car.

I pushed open the door and chased the offender. He only made it three feet before I latched onto his back like a monkey. He stumbled around while I clung on. He finally toppled onto my inch-tall grass.

Out of the corner of my eye, I watched Hagen get out of his truck and sprint toward me. Page intercepted him at the bottom of my driveway.

"Hagen, have some lemonade. This is going to be good." He waited for me to give him the nod before he relaxed and took the lemonade bottle from Page.

I went back to the problem at hand—or *under* hand, as it were.

I grabbed a fistful of sandy-blond hair and slammed his face into the tall grass repeatedly. "You big jerk. Do you even know how bad you scared me?"

A muffled laugh filtered back to me. I dug my knee a little harder into his spine. "I almost peed my pants!"

More cackling laughter from my victim. He wasn't taking this as seriously as he should have. So I did the only thing that would stop him in his tracks.

"Wet Willy."

His laughter turned to shrieks for mercy.

I gave him none.

When I finally stood up, I felt slightly more justified and restored to my normal self. I pulled the man-boy from the grass while Page made introductions to Hagen. "That's our cousin Jordan. He's here for the week—if Kylie doesn't kill him first."

Jordan grinned and flashed a smile. How anyone so annoying had such a contagious grin was beyond me. I wanted to be mad at him for slamming his face against my car window, but now that I wasn't in danger of being a pants-wetter, it was a little funny, especially since he still had tufts of grass stuck to his face.

He leapt toward me and crushed me to his chest. Good grief, being a contractor had done good things for him.

"When did you get so built?"

"Please, I've always looked this good." He stepped back and made a show of flexing. "You're just jealous that you don't have abs like these." He started to grab the hem of his shirt, but I jerked it back down into place.

"There are innocent eyes here. Hagen doesn't need to see that."

He gave me a fake scowl then ruffled my hair, completely ruining any semblance of my low bun.

It was funny how you could love your cousins, siblings, and parents, but some days, you'd be perfectly happy if you could strangle them.

Too bad my hands wouldn't even meet around his neck.

"Next time, I won't be so forgiving," I told him. "Come on, I'll make us some dinner."

Jordan and Page walk-raced each other to the house.

I looked at Hagen, who had an amused smirk on his face. "Another cousin?"

"They're like ants. When one shows up, the others follow."

He folded his arms and stepped his feet shoulder-width apart. "So, I found something interesting this morning."

I copied his stance. I was pretty sure I looked ridiculous. "Oh, really? And what was that?"

"There was a rubber snake waiting for me in my car. It was almost like someone around here found my missing spare key."

"Interesting." I tapped my fingers against my arm.

"That's not the only interesting thing." He gave me a meaningful look. "I also found another plate of muffins. They were delicious. I ate every last one. I didn't even care if they were poisoned. It was worth every bite."

I couldn't have wiped the ridiculous smile off my face if I had tried—and believe me, I tried.

I unfolded my arms and pointed to the house. "I'm making spaghetti and garlic bread for dinner if you're brave enough to join us."

His mouth quirked up in a warm smile that showed his teeth. "Well, I'd hate to be a coward. Lead the way."

Hagen trailed behind me as I walked up to the house.

A long arm reached around me and opened the door for me. He lightly brushed his hand against my back, sending warmth up my spine. He was making me forget why I'd walked into the house. I'd have to do my best to not burn the garlic bread since Hagen was good at distracting me.

Jordan sat at the bar, eating leftover takeout from last week, and Page was sitting there watching it happen with a smirk on her face.

As annoying as Jordan could be, I still didn't wish food poisoning on him. Not to mention, he wouldn't have been much good to me if he was lying on my couch, puking. I had decided that if he was going to be here, I was going to put him to work on my honey-do list.

I knocked the fork from his hand as he started to bring an especially slimy bite of chow mein to his mouth.

"Ask before you eat," I told him as I scooped up the cardboard containers and tossed them in the trash. "That stuff is old. Like, moldy old."

Jordan's face contorted into a grimace. "Why don't you clean out your fridge every once in a while?"

"It keeps pesky cousins away. Now stop eating gross food. I'm making dinner."

"Where's your TV?" Jordan asked as he popped open a can of soda to guzzle.

I pointed to where the TV sat on its stand in the living room. It was clearly visible since my living room and kitchen were open concept.

Jordan looked at it in horror. "That's the size of a computer monitor. I'll need a magnifying glass to watch any games!"

He walked into the living room and fell to his knees like he was dying. I looked at Hagen and rolled my eyes.

"You know, there's a sports bar just down the road," Hagen told him. "Or you all could come to my place this week, and we'll barbecue some steaks and watch it on my TV."

Jordan stood up, a new look of hope in his eyes. "How big is the screen?"

"Eighty-two inches."

"That'll do. I'll bring the drinks. Kylie will bring something delicious to eat. You grill the steaks, though. She always burns them."

The doorbell rang in three short bursts. There was only one person that could have been. Hagen stepped over to the door and opened it. I heard a female voice ask, "Who are you?"

"Who are you?" Hagen shot back.

"Oh, we must have the wrong house. But hey, my very available and single cousin lives in this same neighborhood."

Hagen swung the door wide and pointed to me. "You mean that cousin?"

"Yup, that's the one." Jenny swept into the house— which was more of a polite way to say elephant stampede. Her hair was braided on both sides, and she was wearing her favorite unicorn t-shirt. I was pretty sure she'd had it since middle school. Mack walked in behind her. Mack's real name was Mathias. No kidding. His parents had great hopes he would live up to his serious name. Those hopes had long since been dashed, and we all just called him Mack.

It was a typical entrance from the two of them. Jenny's tiny feet were amazingly loud. I thought she liked to announce her presence, whereas Mack was completely silent. I mean, he actually had the grace of a ballerina, which was shocking because we came up with the nickname "Mack" for a reason.

Jenny hopped onto the counter like she didn't have the

twiggy limbs she inherited from our grandpa. She must have been working out.

Mack leaned in to hug me with his tree-trunk arms. If only he were travel-sized, I would have taken him everywhere as a deterrent to my stalker.

"Kylie, we've missed you," Mack said.

Mack was, hands down, the sweetest of all my cousins. Tenderhearted, he was always the first one to help when someone got injured. As a kid, his family had decided to get rid of a dog that kept biting people. Mack didn't want to give the dog away, so he ran away from home to hide the dog. It had been a full-blown hostage negotiation between Aunt Tricia and Mack.

She lost. Mack kept the dog, and it refused to leave his side the rest of its life. It was the only time I remembered seeing Mack argue with his parents.

"How've you been?" I asked Mack and Jenny.

"We've been good. Busy working. Mom and Dad are trying to find a hobby together. They've taken up golf," Mack said.

"Oh no."

"Yup." He grimaced. "Don't answer their calls unless you want to spend some quality time on the green."

I watched out of the corner of my eye as Hagen glanced between us. To an outsider, it might have sounded like an innocent thing to take up a hobby with your spouse, but it wasn't when it involved Aunt Tricia. I turned to Hagen. "Aunt Tricia and Uncle Mike switch hobbies regularly, and they think everyone else should be just as obsessed with those hobbies as they are. It's like they lock their jaws and try to drag the rest of us down with them."

Hagen answered, "They sound fun."

It sounded like he genuinely meant it. "Well, if you're wanting to take up golfing, I'll text them."

Mack turned to Hagen, too. "If you start golfing with my parents, I'll name my firstborn child after you. I'm running out of excuses not to go."

Hagen walked into the kitchen and snagged another drink out of the fridge. "Hmm, tempting. I don't think anyone's named their future kid after me, but I think I'll have to pass."

"Darn," Mack muttered.

Jenny elbowed past Hagen and began digging around in the fridge. "Anything to eat in here?"

It wasn't even six yet, and everyone acted like they were dying of starvation. Oh well. I secretly loved it. It made me feel needed. I pulled the hamburger out of the fridge and started cooking it on the stove while everyone else sat down at the bar or in the living room. The chatter of voices filled the house, reminding me of all the times we'd spent at each other's houses as kids.

I began humming quietly as I stirred the hamburger.

"Is there a cat dying under the house or is that Kylie singing again?" Jordan called from the couch.

I snagged the towel off of the oven door and walked into the living room where I snapped Jordan on the back of the head.

"Ow."

"Better be nice to the cook," Jenny reminded him.

Hagen watched from his perch on the barstool in amusement. "You sure are a violent little group, aren't you?"

We all turned to stare at him. "It's a requirement to survive in the Boone family."

Hagen smirked. "It explains so much."

"What does that mean?" Jenny asked, leaning forward where she sat on the arm of the couch.

"Nothing!" I said in a singsong voice. Page might have

heard about our little prank war, but that didn't mean everyone else needed to hear about it.

I turned my back on everyone in the living room. I looked at Hagen and made a slicing motion across my neck. His smirk turned downright evil. He walked past me, brushing against my shoulder as he made his way to the living room.

"Let me tell you all about what it's like living next to Kylie."

I glared at him, but he just grinned and said, "Meat's burning."

Sure enough, something was smelling a little scorched on the stove. I dashed into the kitchen and saved dinner. I hoped I'd get it all thrown together before he could tell too many stories. It wasn't like our little feud was one-sided.

Fifteen minutes later, I had the noodles and sauce set out on my island counter. "Time to eat!"

Everyone filed into the kitchen and loaded their plates.

"So, how did your little war start?" Jordan asked around a mouthful of bread.

I glanced at Hagen; he raised his brows and looked at me. I said, "It started over a bunch of garbage."

The rest of the evening was filled with Hagen finding out all sorts of embarrassing things about me from my cousins. Finally, I managed to steer them toward other volatile topics that didn't revolve around me and Hagen: things like MiMi, football, and the upcoming family reunion.

I watched Hagen throughout the evening and noticed that he was happy to sit back and listen, never demanding that the attention be on him. I kept looking at him as though he would have the answer for what I was feeling for him.

Which was true love? The instant kind or the kind that

you struggled and worked for? I needed to call my mom as soon as possible.

"Hey, Hagen, has Kylie ever told you about the time she wrecked my mom's car?" Mack asked with a grin.

It was going to be a long few days. Hopefully, the police caught the person who broke into my house soon. I wasn't sure my pride could handle much more of my cousins.

Chapter Twenty

KYLIE

"*H*i, sweetie. How are you? Did everyone get there this weekend?" Mom smiled at me from the other side of my phone screen. She sat in a deck chair, wearing her sunglasses and sun hat.

"Everyone's here. I had to come talk to you in the garage so I'd have a chance of hearing you."

"Oh, that's why you're sweating."

"Um yeah, it's freaking hot in here."

"You really should get one of those air conditioner units for your garage. I have been loving it ever since Dad installed it. I haven't told the kids about it, so anytime I tell them I'm going to clean the garage, they stay inside the house, and I have some peace and quiet in the garage."

"Of course you did, Mom. Why doesn't that surprise me?" I laughed. I mean, I loved my siblings, but they had some insane talent for driving people crazy. I pulled out a cold bottle of water from my small beverage fridge. I rolled it back and forth across my face and down my neck. "Mom, do you think it's unhealthy if a couple were to fight?"

Mom pulled her sunglasses down her nose and peered into the camera. "Which couple?"

"A hypothetical couple."

"Hmm. Well, I think it depends on the type of fighting you're talking about."

"You know, disagreeing. Like, whether you should buy a black or red car, or if your kids should go to public or private school."

"Then of course a couple should fight!"

"What?" I chugged a drink out of the water bottle. "You and Dad never fight! I've never, ever, ever seen you fight!"

"Sweetie, your dad and I disagree every day of our lives."

I narrowed my eyes and studied her face. "Who are you, and what have you done with my mother?"

She sighed. "Something that was important to me when we started having kids was creating a stable home for you guys. You know I didn't grow up with that, so I wanted you guys to feel secure with your parents."

My mom grew up in a house where divorce was suggested every day if her parents weren't getting along. Coincidentally, my mom's mom had been divorced and remarried four times. Mom didn't even know where her biological dad was anymore. Needless to say, there hadn't been a whole lot of stability during my mother's growing up years.

"Your dad and I were determined to not fight in front of you. But of course we disagreed! Why do you think he had to help me 'change lightbulbs in the bathroom' so often? We were going in there to argue! If a couple isn't arguing about something, then they're either delusional or one of them is trampling all over the other one."

"You mean to tell me that it's normal—even healthy— for a couple to argue?"

"Of course, honey. Maybe not all the time—that would be exhausting—but especially the first few years together, a couple should do some arguing. It helps you find your dynamic as a couple, and it helps you learn more about that person."

"Mom, I've never argued with any of my boyfriends before."

She rolled her eyes. "Yes, all three of them."

"Hey, I put some effort into dating them."

"That's probably why it didn't work out, honey. You shouldn't have to put a bunch of effort into the beginning of a relationship. Besides, you never argued with them, and where are they now?"

"Well, two of them are married, actually... so you know."

"It's because they weren't worth the trouble of arguing with."

"Mom, I'm going to be real honest here: I don't know where you're going with this."

"Someday, you'll find someone that you can argue your point of view with without fear of them leaving you. Did you ever not say something to your boyfriends, or even friends, because you were afraid they wouldn't agree with you and that would be the end of the relationship?"

"Well, yes. Doesn't everybody do that?"

"No, not everybody. You're kindhearted toward people, Kylie, and that's something I love about you. But I don't want you to end up marrying someone who's not going to listen to your voice."

"I guess I hadn't thought of that."

Mom pushed the sun hat back onto her head and brushed some flyaway hairs out of the way. "Look, sweetie, starting a family isn't a race. I know that's what you want, but trust me, you want it with the right guy."

"I know, Mom. I just need to know how to know if it's the right guy or not."

Mom sat up straight, fast enough that her face moved out of the camera lens. "Have you met someone?"

"No! No, I haven't met anyone. I just wanted to know if it's normal to argue."

"You have met someone!"

I hated my mom's superhero ability to read between the lines. I hoped I inherited that from her for when I was raising my own kids.

"Mom. Stop."

"Todd! Come here!"

"No, Mom, do not call Dad over. You guys are on your anniversary trip. I'll hang up on you!"

She laughed evilly. Of course, I would never hang up on my mother. Talk about rude. Plus I'd be afraid she would haunt me the rest of my life if I did.

"Hi, honey!"

My dad's chin filled the screen before he sat down next to Mom.

"We're talking about love," my mom informed him.

Dad started to stand up and walk away, but Mom pulled him back down.

"Kylie's met someone."

"No, I haven't. Dad. Mom's reading into things again."

"She called me asking if it's normal for couples to argue," Mom explained.

Dad nodded then focused in on me with the same brown eyes I inherited. "Fallen for the neighbor, haven't you?"

"Ugh, Dad." I never could get away with anything as a

kid. I didn't know why I expected things to be different as an adult.

"What?" Mom began bouncing up and down in her seat. "How do you know that's who she's talking about?"

He gave her his classic "really?" face before he turned back to me. "Well, I like him. Bring him by so we can meet him in person sometime. I'm going swimming. Love you, pumpkin."

And then Dad ended the call, bless his heart. If he hadn't, I would have been subjected to exactly four hundred and nineteen questions from Mom regarding Hagen, who apparently had their stamp of approval. None of my other three boyfriends had managed to get that— only Hagen, the neighbor who liked to steal my garbage service.

———

Nothing looked out of place as I stepped into my office Monday morning. I shut the door—something I never did —then locked it. I was beginning to think that every shadow was holding some crazy stalker. It was Saturday morning, but I'd forgotten my tablet at the office Thursday night. I figured I might as well get a little work done while I was there.

There was a card sitting on my desk. I pulled out my phone, ready to dial Rick and tell him that this stalking had reached a new level.

Instead, I called Hagen and put the phone on speaker-phone as I reached for the card.

"Hello? Kylie, is everything all right?"

"There's a card on my desk."

"I'm coming over there."

"No, don't do that. I don't want to interrupt your

work." I actually did want him to come over. I didn't want to open it alone.

Silence.

"Okay, fine. I know I'm interrupting by calling you, but I wanted to be talking to someone while I opened this."

I slid a finger into the envelope and ripped it open.

I pulled out the navy card and set it on the desk. "It's blue," I told Hagen.

"What does it say?"

I slowly opened the card, and let out a laugh.

"Are you okay?"

I couldn't answer through my laughter.

"You better answer me right now, or I'm heading over to your office."

"It's— It's—" I gasped for a breath. "It's a thank you card from Jason."

"He signed it? Well, call Rick!"

"No, you don't understand. I'm running a marketing campaign for Jason, and he wrote me a thank-you card along with a lifetime membership to any of his gyms. This is what he was talking about yesterday, not that note in my gym locker."

"Gym locker? Kylie, you're not making any sense."

"I know, I know. I'll tell you all about it when I get home. Thanks for letting me call you. There's nothing to worry about here—just a free gym membership."

"Has anyone told you you're a little crazy?"

"Yes, you."

"I'm hanging up now. I left Jack in the attic, waiting for me. He's scared to death of mice. He's probably paralyzed by fear, thanks to you."

"Oops. Well, thanks anyway."

I hung up the phone and looked at the note.

Poor Jason. I'd called him a crazy stalker and ran away

from him when all he was trying to do was thank me for heading up the campaign.

I picked up my phone and sent him a text.

Me: Jason, thank you for the card and the gym membership! I'm so excited about that. It's wonderful to work on a business that I can wholeheartedly support.

Jason: I'm glad you like it. I wasn't sure when I saw you on Friday.

Me: Sorry about that. I was a little confused that day and didn't know what you were talking about.

Jason: No worries!

I picked up the card and smiled as I propped it against my succulent pot on my desk. Time to get to work.

———

Three days.

My cousins had been here for three whole days. Page and Jenny came with me to the gym on a couple days, and now Jenny and Jason were making plans to go out to dinner. Funny how things work out.

My cousins might have only been here a few days, but somehow, they'd managed to eat all the food in my house, use all my shampoo and toothpaste, and we were down to half a roll of toilet paper. I skipped the gym in favor of going home and taking inventory of everything in the house before I went to the grocery store.

I'd probably have to borrow Dave's utility trailer to haul all the groceries back from the store. I took a quick inventory of the kitchen, and then I opened the bathroom cupboards.

Someone had folded the towels and put them away, but they were crammed in and lumpy. I pulled them out and folded them in thirds—which was the correct way—and then checked under the sink to see what I was low on. Somebody had been using my anti-frizz hair product. We would need to have a little talk about that. It wasn't cheap stuff. I had a separate budget just for anti-frizzing my hair. Thanks for nothing, southern humidity.

"Okay, Mack, you need anything while I'm at the store?" I asked as I passed him in the living room.

"Hey, could you grab me a toothbrush?" Mack asked.

"Did you drop yours in the toilet or something?"

"Nah, I forgot to pack one."

I whipped around to stare at Mack. "You haven't brushed your teeth in three days?"

He waved a hand through the air like he was swatting at a fly. "Of course I've brushed my teeth. I've been using the pink one."

"The pink one?" I stomped across the room so I could get in his face. "You mean you've been using my tooth-brush for three days?"

He smiled, and his glistening white teeth were the confirmation I was looking for.

I ran from the room and frantically searched my bathroom cabinet for the mouthwash. I swallowed a mouthful, hoping it would kill the germs all the way down to my stomach. I took a few deep breaths to fight off a panic attack, and then I headed back to the living room.

Page stood by the front door, fighting a smile, while Mack was trying to look remorseful and failing.

I tossed her the keys. "Want to go cool down the car?"

She caught the keys in one hand and nodded before

she and Jenny headed outside. It was nice to run errands with people for a change. They could each push a grocery cart.

I turned to glare at Mack. It was not nice to think I'd been sharing a toothbrush with that big lug for several days. "No muffins or cookies for you the entire time you're here."

"Not that!" He looked heartbroken. "I'm sorry, I didn't know it was yours."

"Well, you bit the hand that feeds you. I hope you learn to sleep light, otherwise you never know what could happen to you while you stay here." I raised my eyebrows up and down.

"You wouldn't do anything to me, would you Kylie?"

I pretended to study my nails. "I don't know. You wouldn't use my toothbrush, would you?"

Mack stood up and walked out of the house. I followed him onto the porch, curious about what he would do. He walked across the road and pounded on Hagen's door. No one answered.

Mack sat down on Hagen's porch steps and pulled out his phone. Apparently, this was how millennials threw a tantrum.

I refused to feel sorry about hurting his feelings or scaring him. He shouldn't have used my toothbrush. There were certain lines that shouldn't be crossed.

Chapter Twenty-One

KYLIE

Someone knocked on my window.

A scream froze in my throat when I saw the face in the window.

I shoved my book under my pillow before I walked over to the window and slid it open. "What do you want? I was almost asleep."

Hagen ignored me and climbed through my window. I was glad everyone else was asleep in the other rooms on air mattresses. I never would have heard the end of it from them about a "boy" climbing through my window.

"What did you do with my window screen?" I had been trying to keep them in good condition. Apparently, that didn't matter to some people. He was halfway in, so I slid a couple of fingers into the belt loops of his jeans then tugged. He toppled to the ground with a groan. "Thanks for nothing."

"What are you doing here?"

He climbed to his feet and looked around. He made my master bedroom seem tiny. His eyes landed on my bed. "You sleep on a twin?"

I glared at him. Why was everyone so obsessed with the fact that I slept on a twin? "Yes, I sleep on a twin. It's not like I'm seven feet tall and need a custom-sized bed."

He looked at my bed, then at me, and then he snickered.

"Oh, shut up. Why are you in my house?"

"Because Mack is in mine. Have you heard that man snore?"

I couldn't help it. I laughed. I mean, really, it was Hagen's fault for getting so chummy with my cousins. Maybe I should have warned him what they were like, but I figured he'd find out soon enough.

"You've got to get him out. Apologize or something." Hagen was nearly begging.

"What are you going to give me if I get him out?"

"How about I don't strangle you? How does that sound?"

He tried to sound threatening, but that chance was long gone. He wasn't a violent person—something I knew full well.

"I'll get him out of your house in the morning, if you let me drive you somewhere."

I grabbed a sweatshirt out of my dresser drawer and threw it on top of my spaghetti-strap tank top. I grabbed my down blanket off of my papasan and wrapped up in it. Hagen shoved his hands in his pockets and went to stand in front of my bookshelf.

"Okay, it's a deal," he replied absentmindedly.

I'd get my chance to show him that I wasn't as bad of a driver as he thought I was.

He continued staring at my tall shelf. I had old pictures of my growing-up years with my brothers and sisters and all my cousins. There was an unfortunate picture of me as a freshman in high school looking like nothing but a face full of braces. Maybe I could distract him before he noticed.

"So…" I cleared my throat. "Mack's snoring at your house? Why did you let him in?"

He glanced over his shoulder at me with a knowing look. He turned back to study the shelf while he answered me. "I couldn't turn him away. He was sitting on my porch in tears. What was I supposed to do? He fell asleep on my couch. I could hear him snoring while I was in the shower—in my bedroom—with the water running. I thought he was walking through my house with a chainsaw."

I snorted. "He resorted to tears, huh? That's because he was scared I might do something to him in his sleep tonight."

He nodded and moved over to the dresser to look at the pictures there. "I can understand his concern. I'm surprised I have no lasting damage from when you stayed at my house."

"Meh, I prefer psychological damage."

"Tell that to my bloody nose." His glare wasn't very intimidating when I could see his lips twitching. He sauntered over to my twin bed and sat down on the end. He patted the spot next to him. My breath caught as the room seemed to shrink in size.

"Why don't you come sit next to me?"

I swallowed and nodded, making my way to my bed. My body moved automatically. I wanted to be close to him. The bed shifted as I sat down with a little space between us. I could smell his aftershave when he sat that close. I forgot to breathe.

His forearms tensed as he pushed himself back so that he could lean against the wall next to me. "How long can I expect Mack to be at my house?"

I swallowed, trying to fix my dry throat. "Well, he used my toothbrush."

"So, you're saying I should get him a spare key?"

I giggled at that. "Maybe. I didn't mean to hurt his feelings, but I just assumed everyone knew that toothbrushes are sacred things. I refuse to share mine with anyone."

He raised one eyebrow. "Is that because of the braces?"

I reached out and smacked him lightly. "It's impolite to comment on people's middle school years. We will never speak of the braces years again. Understand?"

"Oh, I don't know," he said as he leaned forward and snagged a picture of my family off the dresser then leaned back against the wall again. "This one is especially precious. Half your face is braces."

"Give me that, you big jerk."

He chuckled as I snatched the picture out of his hands. I laid it facedown on top of the dresser.

He patted the mattress. "No wonder you stole my mattress from me; this thing is as hard as a rock. What are you sleeping on, a piece of plywood?"

"My, aren't you just the funniest guy tonight?" I clicked my tongue.

He smiled. "I'm pretty sure that moon chair is more comfortable than this."

"Papasan."

"What?"

I laughed. "It's called a papasan, not a moon chair."

He looked at me like I was crazy and shook his head. "It looks like it will break if I sit in it."

"It's really comfy. I fall asleep reading in it a lot."

His gaze landed on my bookshelf, and again, I wished he would leave and come back later so I'd have a chance to hide any and all embarrassing evidence he could hold against me.

"Are those those vampire books?"

I dropped my head to my knees. "Yes. Guilty pleasure. Sue me."

"I've read them, too."

I lifted my head and found him grinning at me.

"They were better than I expected."

I smiled. Maybe I should have given Hagen a break rather than jumped to conclusions about him. I was treating him the same way he had treated me when we first met. Time to change the subject.

"So, I went in your garage this week."

He looked at me. "I know. You moved my hammer."

"Oh, did I? I didn't realize. I was busy ogling your tools."

"*Ogling* my tools?"

"Yup. I've never seen anything so organized—or shiny, for that matter. I mean, seriously, you should see my dad's garage, or Grandpa's shop. You're lucky to find your way back out again. But looking at your garage makes me wish I knew what to do with all of those gadgets."

He shrugged and studied his hands. "I like keeping things neat. Easier to work with."

Now he was embarrassed? What did he have to be embarrassed about? A pristine garage? Excellent wood-working skills? Oh, yeah, you better believe I snooped around the other half of the garage. A wood coffee table, bench, dresser, and a lamp all sat next to each other. "Did you make all of the stuff in there?"

He glanced at me then back down at his rough hands. "Yeah."

"That's awesome! When you said you could help me

build my pergola, I didn't think you actually had any skills."

His lips twitched up.

"I was wondering if you would miss that coffee table, because it would look perfect in my living room."

At that, he grinned. "You actually like them."

"Of course! I can't believe you made all that stuff. You better look out or you're going to find yourself with your own reality TV show." I meant it, but it almost seemed as though no one else had bothered to tell him that he had talent.

"You're crazy."

"You know, you keep telling me that, and I don't know why."

"Maybe you should start to believe me."

"And maybe you should believe me when I tell you that you've got talent."

Hagen kicked off his tennis shoes and pulled a foot up on the bed.

"Meh, it's just a hobby."

I looked at him in disbelief. "Is that what you call that list of orders tacked to the wall? Because that looked like some serious work."

Hagen shrugged. "I do it in my spare time. Evenings and weekends. It's peaceful."

"Do I need to give you my 'marketing speech for the doubtful business owner'?"

He looked at me in mock horror. "Oh no, not that. Anything but that."

"If you don't take yourself seriously, no one else will, either. But don't take yourself too seriously, or you won't have any fun at it anymore."

"And fun is the most important thing in life?"

I nodded. "Obviously, fun isn't the end all, but people

who enjoy what they do, enjoy going to work every day. They have less stress in their life, which leads to a healthier lifestyle and, overall, a higher level of happiness. So, yeah, I would say enjoying your job is important. It affects every other area of your life."

He tapped his fingers against his knee. "Do you think it's more important for a person to enjoy their job than to make a lot of money at it?"

"Without a doubt."

"But you're in marketing."

"Exactly. Our marketing firm targets smaller businesses. We try to help people make a living off of those jobs they love so much. My favorite client, Hyacinth, has a small quilt and craft shop downtown. She loves creating things, and she has a natural talent—and patience—for teaching people. She's not looking to become a national chain. We simply helped her be discovered by the community."

He nodded. "So you don't think I'm crazy for loving woodworking?"

"It shouldn't matter what I think. But no, I think you're incredibly talented. I think a lot of people would love to have you do custom work for them."

"I enjoy it. I actually get to see the work I've done. Same with when I'm wiring a house. When it's done, I know I've helped provide light and warmth to that house. It's a very tangible thing. I can't work at a desk all day. It makes me feel like I'm going crazy."

I laughed. I sat behind a desk for the majority of the day, but I liked it. I liked getting to be creative with my work and help my clients find a vision for their business.

"So, tell me. Why do you like building stuff? And can you teach me?" I laughed.

Hagen smiled and leaned his head back against the

wall. "Building furniture is like building memories. When I build a dining room table, I'm building something that a family is going to gather around. I'm going to build it strong enough for a toddler to dance on, or kids to play games on. Families build memories around that table, hosting holidays with grandparents and fighting over who gets the last piece of pie. I build porch swings so people can sit out in the sun and make memories together. In my mind, everything has a purpose."

"That's awesome. You better look out, because if I ever show my mother what you can build, she'll be pounding on your door, ordering all the things."

"Is she obsessed with furniture?"

"She's obsessed with making her house look nice. She's great at decorating and likes to find unique pieces, so custom-made furniture is right up her alley."

"She's not the only one who makes her house look nice. Yours is nice and cozy, too. I've even noticed the difference in my living room."

I felt my cheeks flush at the compliment. I did like things to look good, and cozy was the perfect word for it. His compliments mattered to me, probably more than they should have. He was such a different man than the first impression I'd had of him.

"Why did you snap at me when I first came to your door? I didn't ever do anything to you. I hadn't even seen you before."

"I thought you were someone that my sister-in-law was trying to set me up with. All of my friends and my brother and his wife practically did a victory dance when I broke up with my girlfriend Brooke."

I nodded.

"I wasn't ready to date again, but they kept throwing people at me. Some of them weren't much better than

Brooke, either, so I was a little burnt out from having to change my phone number and undergo plastic surgery."

"Har har. Very funny."

"What, you think this nose is real?"

"Oh, did you have to pay them to add that break line there to make you look more rugged?"

"Yes, I decided I looked too perfect without it." He smiled.

"Thank goodness you're not one of those guys who're full of themselves."

We sat in silence for a few minutes before I asked, "How long did you and your girlfriend date?"

"Six months."

"Wow." Good one, Kylie. Great commentary there.

Hagen glanced at me. "It was six months too long."

I cleared my throat. "Why do you say that?"

"Brooke was…well…ambitious. She had places she wanted to go in her life." He pointed his finger at me. "Don't give me that look. I have nothing against ambitious women; it's just that we didn't have the same view on life— or anything, for that matter. I think if you're going to spend the rest of your life with someone, you should agree on the major things. Things like, if you want to have kids or not, or if you should take over your father's company or keep working as an electrician and woodworker."

"Aha," I said. It was all making sense. His second-guessing his career. His needing a second person to affirm his belief in his work. I stretched out on the bed and propped my head in my hand as I looked at him. "She was one of the controlling ones, huh?"

"Yeah." He studied my pale-yellow wall as though it was the most interesting mural in the world. "Sorry for oversharing. No one wants to hear about exes."

"I actually find it therapeutic. I mean, if I learn from

someone else's exes, it means I can be careful to not end up with someone like that in my life."

He glanced down at me and smirked. "You have any exes to speak of?"

"Oh, not so quick. Come on. Help a girl out. What else should I avoid in a future boyfriend?"

Hagen swallowed. "I've…well, I've always wanted a family. I want a wife and kids. I've always wanted to spend my life with someone who wanted kids, too. I was up front about that when we started dating. I don't really do casual dating because I know what I want. I thought that's what she wanted, too. Brooke lied to me. Told me she couldn't wait to have kids with me some day. Talked about it all the time. I figured since we wanted the same things—to take our kids camping, spend time together—we could work out our other issues, and she would get used to my career choice."

He ran a hand over his face. I bit my tongue to keep from interrupting him. I could see where this was going. Anyone who actively convinced someone they were worthless for choosing a blue-collar job had to be the most selfish type of person out there.

"What did she do?"

"Do?"

"Yeah, for work. Where did she work that she thought she was so much better?"

Hagen chuckled humorlessly. "She didn't work. She 'circulated.' Made social connections but didn't have a job."

"My family has a name for that, and it isn't *circulating*. We call it gold-digging."

Hagen reached over and squeezed my hand as he continued. "One night, when she was arguing her point that I needed to take my place on the board at my father's company, she got mad enough that she told me the truth. She wished she had picked my older brother, Branton, instead of me. Then, she told me that she had lied to me about wanting kids and had tied her tubes because she didn't want a baby to ruin her figure, and she for sure wasn't going to 'waste her time adopting a baby.'"

"Thank goodness," I said quietly.

He looked at me in surprise.

I lifted a shoulder and smiled sheepishly. "She's a liar and selfish. Sounds like she'd be a terrible mother."

His lips parted and then slowly stretched into a smile. "Thank you for that. It feels good to tell someone what happened."

"You mean you haven't told anyone?"

He shook his head. "I just tell them it was irreconcilable differences."

"I'll say. She was a liar and a selfish witch. How did you end up with someone like that?"

"She was charming in the beginning. Smart. She seemed kind. Turns out, she just wanted a piece of the family business."

"What exactly does your family do?"

"Dad owns Glacier Bank."

"Oh, he's one of the branch owners?"

Hagen smirked and shook his head. "No, he owns the chain."

The chain. Glacier Bank had at least fifty locations in Louisiana alone. I didn't know how much money we were talking about, but I had a feeling being a bank owner wasn't in the same pay grade as being a marketing team manager.

I waited for this information to change what I thought of Hagen. Nothing happened. He was still the attractive man sitting on my twin bed, teasing me about books, and talking about an ex-girlfriend. I licked my dry lips. "Oh—okay. That is not what I expected you to say."

"That my parents have money?"

"I was hoping you were going to say they owned an adventure park or a vacation resort. Page is right; I need some friend perks here. Banks are just boring. Money everywhere. How plebeian."

He grinned at me and squeezed my leg, sending an electric wave up my skin. "You're hopeless."

We spent the next couple hours swapping stories and insults. I told him about my big, crazy family and complained about working with Lyle. He told me about his mom trying to get more grandbabies. It felt so natural to be sitting on my small bed with him. We gravitated closer together as we showed off our childhood scars along with the stories of how we got them. After that particular conversation, we didn't move apart. We simply sat there, leaning against each other. He asked about my cactus that had been named Landon, so I told him all about it.

"Kylie."

"Hmm?" I was pretty comfy, curled up against his side, letting him play with my hair.

"Let's go on a date."

I opened my eyes to look at his face. He looked serious, but I wasn't sure. "You mean a real date?"

"Yeah, a real date. Dinner, flowers, the whole works. And you can't use Landon as an excuse. If you don't want to go on a date, all you have to do is tell me no, and I'll respect that."

"Are you sure that's a good idea?" My heart continued its irregular beating as I waited for his answer.

He shook his head. "I don't know. But I'd like to try. I like you. I know I shouldn't have been so rude to you when you came to my door. But I'm not sorry about our little war. It's the most fun I've had in a long, long time."

I smiled at that because the same was true for me. "Okay. Let's go on a date."

———

I was buried under a pile of blankets, wrapped up like a taco. The last thing I remembered was Hagen running his hands through my hair until my eyes drifted closed. My phone was ringing, and I quickly picked it up.

"Hello?"

I glanced around. Hagen had left sometime in the night, or maybe early morning, because I didn't even notice him leave. I'd probably been dead to the world and sleeping in a puddle of my own drool.

"Hi, Kylie. This is Rick."

"How are you?"

"Really great. Say, sorry to bother you so early."

I glanced at the time—seven in the morning.

Rick continued. "I'm calling with some good news. We caught the man who's been breaking in to houses around there. He's in custody right now and has already been interrogated and admits to casing a variety of houses in your neighborhood."

"What a relief!" I sank onto my papasan chair but miscalculated and the whole chair ended up tipping over with me in it.

"Are you okay? I heard a crash," he asked.

"I'm fine. Just fell out of a chair."

"No coffee yet, huh?"

"Nope. But hey, thank you for calling. That puts my mind to rest so much. Do you think he's the one who's been sending me notes?"

I could hear a horn in the background and could only assume Rick was commuting through town as he spoke to me. "I think it's a pretty good bet he's the one. I don't want to disturb you, but he made several comments about how beautiful you were. He said he got distracted when he was casing your house, because he enjoyed watching you so much."

Now I was going to have to take out a personal loan to pay for a twenty-foot-tall privacy fence around my house. Creepers who talked about loving to watch you didn't exactly inspire confidence in me.

"I'm sorry that we didn't make the connection between those notes and the break-ins sooner. I'm hoping we'll get a full confession from him today. It will make it easier to move forward to a trial. If you want, you could bring in those notes and press charges and get a restraining order. He's not going to make bail, though, because he's a flight risk."

I sighed. "As long as he's not getting out anytime soon, I'm happy to leave it alone."

"Alright. Well, you have a good day, and I'll keep you updated on any changes with the case."

"Thanks, Rick."

I hung up the phone and leaned back in the chair —carefully.

My stalker days were over. No more notes, pictures, or break-ins.

Chapter Twenty-Two

HAGEN

I was obsessed with Kylie. It was official. I snuck over to her house just to talk with her the night before because I missed her so much. It was sad to see her go. I'd enjoyed having her stay with me, and while I was busy looking both ways before I entered a room still, I loved it.

I sat at my bar, sipping coffee, while I listened to Mack snore. I didn't enjoy his company nearly as much as I did Kylie's. Talking with her last night had been cathartic.

When we'd talked about life aspirations, she listened to what I wanted to do, rather than projected what she thought I should do in my life. It had been a breath of fresh air to feel someone's support like that. It was sincere; she didn't get anything out of supporting my dreams. That was what made it mean so much more. When I told her who my family was, she didn't get starry-eyed with money signs.

From the minute Brooke was in my life, she had tried to control it. First in small things, like where we went on dates and who we went to dinner with. She refused to eat at a restaurant without a tablecloth, and usually, our dinner mates were potential business partners.

Her controlling nature revealed itself when she began telling me I needed to change careers. What she really wanted was the Raglund money.

My phone chimed with a text from Rick.

Rick: Caught the guy who broke into Kylie's. Pretty sure he's the one who was sending notes too. I'll keep you guys updated.

Victory dance. There was nothing standing in the way of us going out on a date. No more people doubting my work; no more trying to live my life the way other people thought I should; no more worrying about Kylie being stalked.

The downside was that now I didn't have an excuse to always be checking in on Kylie. Hopefully, we could have a seamless transition from helpful neighbor to hovering boyfriend.

Because I was pretty sure I would turn out to be a hoverer. When I was dating Brooke, I didn't really care what she was up to. Toward the end, I was relieved when she wasn't around. But with Kylie, I found myself worrying about her all the time. I wanted to be there to hear about her day at work. I wanted to help her build that pergola. I wanted to put my arm around her in public. I wanted to sit at the table and eat muffins while I listened to her ramble about her job and sing off-key.

I even wanted to walk out of my house a little nervous at what prank she would try to pull next. Now that she had told me yes about going out with me, I had the chance to do this right. Come what may, I was going to make her happy. No matter what it took.

The first thing I needed to do was kick Mack out of my house.

———

Kylie and her cousins were coming over to barbecue, along with my brother, Alex, and his wife, Linley. Most likely the devil baby, Mia, too. It was our way of celebrating that the burglar had been caught. I had no idea if I had enough food set out, but I hoped so. I started warming up the briquets before I went inside and began assembling the food. My front door opened, and Page marched inside as though she had known me her entire life. I expected no less from her.

"Everyone else will be here in a minute. Mack was busy apologizing to Kylie and trying to sneak a muffin."

She plopped down on the counter next to the food. She snatched a piece of pineapple from where I was cutting it. "So, Kylie told me about the pancakes. Are we sure you should be barbecuing?"

I pointed the knife at her. "I might not be a breakfast cook—and I still blame the pancake mix—but I refuse to let anyone take my barbecue title from me. Wait until you try some of my food." I winked at her and carried the trays outside. She followed behind, munching on more pineapple.

"Wait, are we eating that squash raw?"

"Just trust me. Kylie might be able to cook and bake, but I know my way around a barbecue." I set the food down on the tall, wooden table I had built to use as a barbecue counter. "Why don't you make yourself useful and hook up those misting sprinklers?" I pointed to the corner of the patio.

For some reason, Page felt like the little sister that I never wanted. It was great. She was easy to be around, snarky, and I wasn't attracted to her at all. Unlike Kylie, who managed to keep my head spinning whenever she entered a room.

I dumped the hot coals out of the chimney onto the grill.

"Wow, you even barbecue like a real man."

"Quiet with the spectators."

"Have a nice time with Kylie last night?"

I glanced over my shoulder at her. I hadn't thought anyone else was awake last night.

She pointed the hose at me as she waited for an answer. I ignored her and slapped the steaks onto the grill.

"I know that you know that I know that you like her."

I salted the veggies on the tray before I answered her. "I have no idea what you just said, but I wouldn't worry about it if I were you."

"Why not? She's my cousin. And if you couldn't tell, she's the sweetest one of us all. She...well, she's more soft-hearted than the rest of us."

I smirked. "I know. That's why I like her. Besides, we're going on a date Friday."

She dropped the sprinkler on her foot. "Ouch!"

"You okay?" I asked as I tossed the veggies on the grill.

"That sneak. She didn't even say a word this morning."

"Who didn't say a word?"

We spun around and looked at the back door. Kylie stood there, holding a plate of cupcakes.

"Who didn't say a word?" Kylie asked again as Mack, Jordan, and Jenny filed out of the house.

"You didn't say anything about going on a date with Hagen!" Page accused her.

Kylie blushed when she glanced at me, and Jordan whistled loudly in her ear. Everyone else started talking over one another.

No wonder she didn't tell them first thing this morning.

Someone started pounding on my back and telling me congratulations. You would've thought we'd just told them we were getting married in Hawaii and they were all invited.

"What smells so good?" Kylie asked over the noise.

Everyone stopped their teasing and circled around the barbecue. "Did you build this barbecue yourself?" Mack asked.

"Yup. You can never find one big enough."

"I'm pretty sure you could barbecue a whole cow on this thing. It's great," Mack said.

"What are you doing?" Jenny asked.

I pulled the steaks off and covered them with foil, then threw the pineapple rounds on the grill and tossed the squash on. I grabbed the slices of bread and dropped them on the grill. "What's it look like I'm doing?"

"It looks like you don't know what you're doing," Jenny said as she swiped a piece of bread off the hot barbecue and shoved it in her mouth. I couldn't help but be impressed that she managed to eat it in one bite.

"Wow, this is delicious," she mumbled around the bread.

I glanced around and realized Kylie wasn't outside anymore. A couple minutes later, I pulled everything off the grill, and the cousins began loading their plates. I headed inside and found Kylie setting out muffins on a plate in the kitchen.

She wasn't alone.

Alex and Linley sat on the barstools across from her. The baby was strangely absent.

"I wasn't sure you guys would stop by. Where's the siren?"

"Sleeping on your bed."

"Everyone seems to like sleeping on my bed." I glanced at Kylie and couldn't stop my grin when I saw her blush.

"We've been chatting with your nice neighbor. Things were a little crazy the first time we met," Linley continued.

"So, how did you guys end up being friends with this grumpy bear?" Kylie asked as she began mixing a pitcher of lemonade. She must have brought that over, because I knew for sure I didn't have anything in my house to make lemonade with.

Alex laughed. "Him? We didn't have a choice."

I smiled as I grabbed a muffin and took a big bite of it. Lemon. "Who are you kidding? I was there first. I was the one who got stuck with you."

Kylie glanced back and forth between us with a confused look on her face.

"Alex is my little brother," I explained.

"Oh! Oh, I should have noticed the resemblance."

We all laughed at that one. Alex's mahogany skin and my tan but freckled skin didn't scream blood-related.

"That twerp invaded the family when I was four. He was such a pain growing up, and now he's all Linley's problem. Always a suck-up. He could do no wrong in Mom and Dad's eyes. But I knew the truth: he was a pain in the you-know-what. It's Linley's job to keep him out of trouble now." I loved teasing my brother about—well, anything.

"Don't worry, Linley gives me time off for good behavior and lets me come over here and harass him whenever I want." He shrugged.

Kylie nodded. She had a serious look on her face when

she pointed at him and said, "You and I need to have a talk later. I could use some inside information."

I glared at her then pointed at Alex. "You two, outside with everyone else. Kylie and I need to talk."

"Okay, Dad," Alex said as he draped an arm around Linley's shoulders and headed outside. "Let us know if you hear the baby crying!"

I waited for the back door to swing shut before I spun to face Kylie.

She held the sprayer nozzle from the sink in her hand. She squeezed the trigger. It was a direct hit to my chest.

"You did not just—"

She shrugged. "You looked like you needed to cool down a little."

I savored the look of terror in her eyes when I advanced on her. She tried to keep the nozzle out of my reach, but my arms were decidedly longer than hers, and I had her trapped with her back to the sink.

I snatched the nozzle from her hand before she could do any more damage and set it back in the sink. I braced a hand on either side of her on the counter and leaned in until our foreheads were touching. "You can't seem to stay out of trouble, can you, brace face?"

She groaned. "Aren't you going to forget you ever saw those pictures?"

"Are you going to stop spraying me with water and shooting me with paintball guns?"

I could tell she was fighting a grin when she shook her head. We were so close I could smell her shampoo. Vanilla. I'd never known something so simple could smell so good.

I had to get a grip on myself before Page marched through the door and tore my arms off. I brushed my fingers against Kylie's slender wrist as I found my way to her waist. "You're not going to back out on our date, are you?"

She shook her head and swallowed. "I'm looking forward to it."

I smiled and settled my other hand on her waist. "Me too."

"Do you think my cousins are scaring your brother away?"

"They're probably all plotting how to make my life miserable." I leaned closer until my nose brushed hers.

Her breath caught, and she rested her hands on my shoulders. She flexed her fingers lightly, drawing me closer. Her uneven breathing matched mine.

I hadn't planned on our first kiss being in my kitchen, me wearing a wet t-shirt while our families were outside being as loud as possible. I wanted to make it a memorable event. Maybe walking on the waterfront in the dark. Maybe underneath the Fourth of July fireworks. Something that would show her how serious I was about us.

Now that we were here, though, I didn't think I could stop myself.

But then she was the one to make the move.

She tilted her head back and brushed her lips against mine. All bets were off. Forget the perfect first kiss setting. My kitchen had never seemed so romantic. I raised a hand to the back of her neck as I pressed closer. I nipped at her lips with mine before I deepened the kiss. As crazy as she was making me, I didn't want to scare her away.

I didn't need to worry about that. She parted her lips and angled her head to the side. That was all the invitation I needed.

"Boo! Get a room!" someone yelled. The baby started crying, and a door slammed.

I pulled away slowly and glanced over my shoulder. Jenny and Mack stood there, grinning.

"Just for that, you get to go get the baby," I told them.

Kylie buried her face into my chest, and I could feel her rapid breaths warm against my chest.

Mack and Jenny stared at the bedroom door that held the crying baby. I was perfectly happy to stand right where I was with Kylie still in my arms.

"Have at it, guys."

Mack pulled his shoulders back and marched down the hall while Jenny made a quick escape outside.

Without letting Kylie go, I turned both of us to watch as Mack disappeared into my bedroom. He came back out carrying a curly-haired baby that stared at him in awe. She looked tiny in his arms. There was something about being held by a tank of a man that made her seem minuscule. She reached up and patted his face then grabbed his lips and pulled.

"Ouch."

I kept my arm around Kylie, and we followed Mack out the back door. He headed straight for Linley and tried to hand Mia to her.

Mia would have none of it. She grabbed Mack's ears, one in each fist, and clung on. He straightened and tried again, but she started to wail. Mack shrugged and tucked Mia into his left arm and went over to load himself a plate.

"The babies always love Mack. Every time we have a family get-together, it's always the babies and toddlers that go find him. I guess they just feel safe with him," Kylie explained.

"You'd think they'd be terrified. I know I am."

She laughed. "Oh, he can be terrifying when he's mad, but it usually only happens once every few years. It takes a lot to make Mack angry. Any other time, he's a big softie."

"You did make him cry about the whole toothbrush incident."

Kylie shrugged. "I know how to terrorize him. Comes with the territory of growing up with lots of cousins."

"Hmm, I think you could find a way to terrorize anyone. You know, I've had to start buying bottled water. I swear I can still taste that vinegar you put in the water pitcher."

Kylie giggled. "You had that coming, garbage thief."

Chapter Twenty-Three

KYLIE

*D*ate night. I'd never been so nervous and excited at the same time. Hagen had told me to dress casual, so I was wearing an off-the-shoulder sundress with wedge sandals.

The doorbell rang, and Page raced past me, holding my baseball bat.

She swung the door open and greeted Hagen.

"That must be the Boone family weapon of choice."

She grinned and lifted the bat. "Either this or a golf club."

"Did I do something to make you mad?"

"Nah, I just figured since Kylie's dad wasn't here to meet you with a shotgun, I'd do the honors with Kylie's bat."

"Is this the part where you tell me to have her back by nine?"

"Oh no, I'm much more progressive than that."

"Thank goodness, I was worried."

"You can have her back by ten."

I bit my cheek to keep from laughing as Hagen nodded solemnly. "I promise."

"Okay, you can come in."

Hagen walked through the door, and he smiled when he saw me. His eyes never left mine. "You look great."

He leaned down and kissed my cheek. I smiled and nodded. "You do, too."

Something crashed, breaking us out of our trance.

"What. Is. Happening?"

He grasped my hand as we both stared at the disaster that used to be my kitchen.

"I bet them they couldn't make a well-rounded dinner while I was gone tonight."

Jordan and Mack were busy trying to put out a fire on the stove. Jenny had a knife and was chopping carrots so fast that they were flying around the kitchen like missiles. Page was now busy trying to direct everyone in the kitchen using the baseball bat and accidentally knocked over an open can of tomato sauce, sending it flying across the floor.

"I'm a little worried about your house."

"I promised them I'd set MiMi on them."

"What's a MiMi? Wait, is this the grandma you were talking about the other night?"

"Yup, that's the one. Nothing scarier than my grandma."

"If you say that, then I think I might be terrified to meet her."

"Nah, you'll get along just fine. She likes people who say it like it is."

A pot crashed to the ground, and Hagen put his hand on my lower back. "Let's get out of here before you get the urge to clean something."

He took me to a local pub on the waterfront in Lampton. I'd been there once before and loved it. He couldn't have picked a better restaurant for our first date. I loved dressing up as much as the next girl, but I wanted to spend more time with the relaxed Hagen that I'd come to know over the past couple weeks.

Hagen held out my chair for me then ordered us drinks and appetizers. After the waiter left, he unzipped his sweatshirt and peeled it off of his arms. You'd better believe I watched. That man had some nice arms. It would have been ungrateful of me to not show some appreciation.

I couldn't be positive, but it seemed like he flexed a little as he turned around and rested his arms on the table once more.

He had a funny expression on his face, as though he was trying not to laugh.

Then I glanced down.

He was wearing a graphic t-shirt. It had a picture of a smiling potted cactus on it.

I laugh-snorted. He grinned.

"I thought you'd be more comfortable if you felt like you were out with an old friend."

I couldn't stop smiling. He was wearing a cactus shirt for me. Where did a person even find that kind of thing?

"I've got to tell you, after reading the reviews on this t-shirt, I keep waiting for something miraculous to happen."

My cheeks were starting to hurt from my new permanent grin. "What do you mean?"

"I always read the reviews before I buy something. When I read the reviews for this shirt, they said it was guaranteed to be a 'chick magnet.'"

"Please tell me those aren't the words that were used."

He smiled. "Oh, they were. I took a screenshot of that review. I'll send it to you so you can enjoy it, too."

It hurt trying to hold my laughter in.

"Okay, I have a question."

His smile dropped at my serious tone. "Alright."

"You said you read reviews before buying anything."

"Yes..."

I sipped my sweet tea. "What's it like grocery shopping with you?"

He didn't blink, didn't give anything away. "Very thorough."

"And I thought shopping at the hardware store with you was bad."

"Oh, you haven't seen anything yet."

Eating dinner with Hagen was turning out to be quite a workout with all the laughing I was doing.

After dinner, he asked if I wanted to walk down the boardwalk. There were supposed to be some musicians performing near the small park close to the waterfront.

He held the door for me as we left the restaurant then grasped my hand as we walked down the boardwalk. It was a beautiful night along the river. He held his sweatshirt in one hand and my hand in the other. I hadn't really thought about why he would have been wearing a sweatshirt when he showed up to my house, but now it made perfect sense. Every time I looked at that cactus on his shirt, it made me want to burst out laughing. It was such a thoughtful thing. It meant he'd actually been paying attention when I was talking to him.

The streetlights made it easy to see where we were walking. The restaurants and shops that lined the board-walk in Lampton were picturesque.

We were walking past the nicest restaurant in town. Jean Guyre's. White tablecloths, candles, black-tie waiters. I couldn't have been happier that Hagen had taken me to a pub. If we had gone to a restaurant like Jean Guyre's, it would have felt so formal, so stiff. Instead, we got to talk about things like cactus shirts and his ability to eat a crazy amount of beer-battered fries. I'd had a great time and was already looking forward to a future date with him.

The door to Jean Guyre's opened, and four women stepped out. They were all tall, blonde, and thin. It was like we had bumped into a model convention.

Hagen squeezed my hand tight and pulled me to the edge of the boardwalk. He sped up as he maneuvered us around the women.

We blazed past, and I was fairly certain my cheeks were getting windburned.

"Hagen!"

I glanced over my shoulder and saw one of the blondes calling to us.

"Umm, I think they know you," I told Hagen.

"Keep walking," he muttered.

"Hagen! Wait." The voice was loud and sounded close. I glanced over my shoulder to see an especially tall woman wearing a sleek black dress with matching black clutch. She was disgustingly elegant. Heavy makeup, but done in a way that suggested she looked good even without it.

She had a smile on her face, but the look in her eye was cold. Ice cold. I was pretty sure Hagen would have kept walking if she hadn't latched onto his other arm with her slender, manicured hand.

If I had seen people speed-walking past me, I would have assumed they didn't want to talk. Heck, if my own mother waved at me, I still checked behind me to make sure she was waving at me. I did not, by any means, run down the sidewalk, chasing after a man and his date when they had done their best to avoid me.

But this woman didn't seem phased at all.

"I'm so glad you saw me, Hagen."

Wait, what? Hagen had started training for sprints when

she'd called out to him. He hadn't exactly been flagging the woman down.

"Have a nice night," Hagen said in a way that could have also been telling her to drop dead.

She laughed quietly. "So, who is your little friend? Aren't you going to introduce me?"

I straightened my shoulders back and plastered an equally plastic smile on my face. "I'm Kylie."

Her smile turned positively lethal. "I'm Brooke. I'm sure you've heard all about me."

I bit my tongue to keep from exclaiming about her being Hagen's ex-girlfriend. "Hmm, that does sound familiar." I pretended to be searching for a recollection of her name. "Where do you work? That might help me place you."

She dropped the smile completely, and Hagen rubbed a hand over his mouth.

"Hagen and I have been together a long time. We're just taking a little break right now." She said it with such a straight face that I was certain she believed her own lie.

"That's nice."

"Is this that cousin you were telling me about, Hagen?"

"Brooke, this is my date. Goodnight." He wrapped a protective arm over my shoulders and urged me forward again.

"Give me a call when you get home tonight. You're smarter than Branton. Your parents are excited to have you in the business. I've already hired the decorator for your new office."

"Wow, she's really a treat," I whispered to Hagen as we walked away.

"Delusional."

I glanced at him. He looked angry. I couldn't blame him. I was angry, too. Angry for him. Angry that somehow she still had a hold on his family. Angry that she could act so serene when she was so crazy. Angry that she still affected Hagen.

"You know," I told him as I let go of his hand and instead looped my arm around his. "They say it's the ones who look normal on the outside that are the most crazy on the inside. I, personally, have not been around very many normal people in my life, so I feel like I can check that off my list now."

Hagen snorted. "You know you're crazy, right?"

"Yes, which means I'm perfectly normal. Now, if I thought I was normal, like Brooke obviously does, then I would be worried."

Hagen chuckled stiffly and wrapped his arm around my shoulders. He kissed the top of my head. "Thanks for cheering me up. I'm sorry she ruined our night."

"She didn't ruin our night. I've had a great time."

Hagen sighed as we made our way to the truck. "I wish she would stay away from my family. I've been avoiding them because all they talk about is Brooke and how they want us to get back together."

Hagen opened the door for me, placing a hand on my waist to help me into the truck. It wasn't easy to climb up in a dress.

The drive home was the most awkward moment of the night. I watched as Hagen receded into himself.

At first, he responded to my attempts at conversation with a nod or a small smile. Then, it was a small blink. I realized he wasn't even listening right around the part where I offered to reorganize his garage and he'd readily agreed with a nod. I stopped trying to draw him out. Whatever was going on in his mind was something he was going to have to work through on his own.

That was the trouble with caring about someone. You

couldn't fix everything for them. While I could plainly see Brooke's toxicity, I couldn't force Hagen to see it for what it was. He had been with her for a long time. She had a hold on his family. Of course he would feel drawn to her.

I didn't want to imagine him getting back together with her. He had seemed so miserable when he first moved to this neighborhood. I wanted him to be happy. He had seemed happy with me, but if I tried to force him to be with me, would I have been any different than Brooke?

Hagen backed into his driveway and shut the truck off.

He turned in his seat to look at me. "I had a nice time tonight."

"So did I. But why do I feel like you're about to say something else?"

He sighed. "Because I am. I can't give you more."

"What does that mean?"

"I can't pretend to be different than I am. I really like you, Kylie. That's why I want more for you. You need someone who wants those things."

I held my hand in the air. "Hold up. I'm pretty sure I know what I want in life, and it has nothing to do with how much money a person makes or where he is socially."

Hagen shook his head slowly. "I know you're not like that, but you deserve better."

Now I was getting mad. "Shouldn't I decide what I want more of? You're making this decision as if I'm just like Brooke. Have I ever made you feel like you're less?"

"No, and that's exactly what I mean!"

"So you want me to be a jerk to you?"

"No." Hagen ran a hand over his face. "It's because you're such a good woman that I want you to have the best. I want you to have everything, and I can't give you that world. I don't want to be a part of my parents' world."

I tapped my fingers against my knees.

"Say something," Hagen whispered.

I nodded and kept tapping away on my knees.

"Please."

I turned to glare at him. "I'll say something. I think you're crazy, and I'd like to strangle you—and maybe your crazy ex-girlfriend, too. Let me see if I've got this right. You like me, but basically, you think you're not ambitious enough to give me the life I want."

"You deserve more."

"What if I just want to see where this takes us?"

"You deserve the best in life."

"I think that there are a lot of things better in life than money and social standing. Love, family, adventures, a place to belong."

Hagen smiled and reached across the middle console to squeeze my hand. "You're amazing, Kylie Boone."

I glared at him. "I feel like stuffing you in my garbage can right now."

He rubbed a hand against his forehead. "Maybe I rushed into this. Maybe I just need some time to deal with what happened with Brooke. I like you a lot, Kylie, but right now, I'm too focused on what I'm not."

I sighed. "Well, when you figure out what you are, you can find me across the street. Probably eating muffins."

Chapter Twenty-Four

HAGEN

I'd enjoyed every part of my date with Kylie—up until we ran into Brooke and all of her opinions brought my insecurities back to mind. I spent all of the next day in my garage, working on my special order list.

Seeing Brooke reminded me that I had some unfinished business—with myself as well as my family. I needed time to sort those things out. I didn't want to give Kylie half of myself. I wanted to give her everything. I couldn't do that if Brooke still had a hold on my life. I continued working as I tried to decide the best way to move forward from Brooke. It wasn't as if she held my emotions anymore. I didn't love her. I didn't think I ever did.

When I came back inside to grab a drink, there was a woman standing in my kitchen. She wore a beige, fitted dress and her favorite pearl necklace.

"Hello, dear."

"Hi, Mom."

"What are you doing here?"

"Can't a mother come by to say hello to her son?"

I looked at her. She was trying to give off her best

innocent face. It wasn't working. Mom had always lost on family poker nights.

"What do you really want? You would have invited me out to breakfast or lunch if there wasn't an ulterior motive."

She tapped her hand against the island top.

"I'm sixty years old."

"Yes, I know, Mom."

"I was talking to Brooke this week."

"I don't know what this has to do with me."

"I want grandchildren. You two made such a lovely couple."

I turned around, pulled open the fridge, and grabbed a water bottle. I'd made the switch after Kylie filled my water pitcher with vinegar. That was a rude awakening.

"Mom, there were some things that couldn't be resolved." Like the fact that she didn't love me. Honestly, I tried not to hold that against her because it was apparent the only person she was capable of loving was herself.

"Brooke cares about you. She wants to get back together with you. You could join your father at work and spend more time with us."

"Mom, I've told you. I'm not going to work with Dad."

"Is it so hard to believe we want you there?"

I softened. "No, Mom, and I appreciate that you want me to be a part of the family business, but I already have a career."

"Wiring houses? Honey, you could own those houses!"

"Mom! I. Don't. Want. To."

She sniffed. "You don't have to snap at me, you know."

I rubbed my thumb in the middle of my forehead. I was twenty-eight years old, but I sounded like a hormonal teenager. "I'm sorry I snapped, Mom, but I wish you would leave it alone. I'm happy."

"How can you be happy?! You're not part of the family business. You don't have someone to spend the rest of your life with."

I started to reply, but she cut me off.

"Don't pretend you don't want that. You've told me yourself that you want your own family someday."

I nodded. She wasn't wrong. I just didn't like the way she was trying to "help" me.

"Why don't you work out those differences with Brooke? She likes our family. She loves going to get-togethers with us. She even likes going to the country club luncheons with me! You've seemed so withdrawn the past few months. I want you to be happy."

I nodded because Mom was right. The last couple months that Brooke and I had been together had been straight up miserable, and it took me another couple months—and Kylie—to pull out of my funk.

Mom sighed. "I've always wanted a daughter, too."

I rolled my eyes. "Mom, you have Linley."

"Linley prefers to go on hikes and spend time outdoors. I want one that likes air conditioning as much as I do."

"Mom, someday I'll find someone to spend the rest of my life with." I glanced out my front window and noticed Kylie out mowing her yard. "But it will be someone that accepts me for who I am."

Our talk was interrupted by a blood-curdling scream that came from across the street. I dashed to the front door and stepped out onto my porch. Jordan and Page each had a paintball gun in their hands, and it looked like Jordan was the one screaming for mercy.

Jenny was sitting on the roof with a paintball gun of her own, shooting both Jordan and Page.

My mom's jaw nearly hit her chest. "What is going on out there?"

I grinned. "Just the neighbors."

We watched as Kylie shut off the mower, marched over and took the paintball guns away from Jordan and Page, and pointed at the front door of her house. They walked inside with their heads hanging. Next, she went over and shook her finger at Jenny, who then grabbed the edge of the roof and lowered herself to the ground—remarkably athletic if you asked me. She handed over her paintball gun before heading inside, too.

My mom glanced between me and Kylie's house. "Sweetie, with neighbors like that, I think we could find you a quieter neighborhood than this one."

I shook my head. "Nope. This is the one for me."

She watched Kylie start up the lawn mower again. "I think I see."

I really hoped she didn't. That last thing I wanted was for her to tell Brooke more about Kylie and me. It had nothing to do with me being ashamed of Kylie. I wanted to protect her from Brooke's venomous attitude. She didn't deserve any backlash from Brooke—and there would be backlash. Seeing Brooke last night had shown me just how much I had let her weasel her way into my family. I wouldn't let her turn her sights onto Kylie.

"I've got to run, dear, but be sure to stop by for Sunday lunch. We miss you."

"Okay, Mom. It was good seeing you." Maybe I would show up for Sunday lunch. Maybe it was time to lay all my cards on the table for my parents. I knew they loved me in their own, distant way. I also knew Brooke was an excellent manipulator. Brooke's delusional words last night had shown me it was time to tell my family everything. Maybe it would be the final step to kicking Brooke out of my life for good.

When I stepped outside to turn on my yard sprinklers, I saw Kylie's cousins carrying bags outside to their cars.

Not that I wanted to admit it to myself, but I had gotten a little attached to those crazy cousins of Kylie's. I liked them—as long as Mack wasn't sleeping in my house. It surprised me that everyone had managed to sleep in the same house as that man.

"Hey, Hagen! You coming to the family reunion?" Jenny asked.

I crossed the street without looking. I was sure one of these days I would get run over, but living at the end of the street had its advantages.

"What family reunion?"

"The Boone family reunion, of course," Jenny continued as she hefted a duffel bag as big as her into the back of the trunk.

"Is that Page you have stuffed in there?"

Jenny turned around and grinned at me. "Don't tempt me. So, are you in?"

"I hate to break it to you, but I don't think I'd fit in that bag."

She rolled her eyes. "Well, the reunion's in September, so you'd better be there. MiMi wants to meet you."

I frowned at Jenny. "How does MiMi know about me already?"

"No secrets in the Boone family. It's like we have a permanent group text going on where we share tidbits of gossip about each other."

"Kylie didn't say anything about the family reunion, so I probably won't be there."

"Aw, come on, man." Jordan came up behind me and slung an arm around my shoulder. I lifted it over my head and dropped it. "You've got to come to the reunion. How are you at redneck golf?"

"I'm decent at golf. My dad took it up as a hobby."

Jordan and Jenny glanced at each other and grinned. "Well, playing golf is a little different in the Boone family."

"Did I hear you say something about golf?" Dave, Kylie's neighbor, stood up from behind the hedge he was trimming alongside Kylie's driveway. "I love golfing. I've been looking for a golf buddy."

He looked at us expectantly, as though he were waiting for us to volunteer to go golfing with him.

"I'm afraid I don't have a whole lot of time to golf right now, Dave," I told him. "Maybe when work is a little slower, we could go hit a few rounds."

The offer was out of my mouth before I could pull it back. It must have been Dave's lonely face and the fact that he let Kylie borrow any tool from his garage that made me agree to go golfing with him.

His face lit up, and he dropped his pruning shears. "That's great! We'll plan on it. There's a golf course I've heard has become a little bit of a novelty. It's called The Garden. It's become popular in the last couple months. You just let me know when you want to go."

"Alright. I'll do that."

Dave grinned then headed back up to his house, leaving the shears laying in the yard.

"You realize you'll probably be playing golf for the rest of your life with him?" Jenny whispered loudly.

I shrugged. "That's okay. He's been a decent neighbor."

Jenny smiled at that. "Unlike Kylie, you mean?"

"What's unlike Kylie?" Page asked as she and Mack carried their bags out to the cars. Kylie followed behind, carrying a small bag.

"I told Jenny that Dave has been a good neighbor—unlike some people we all know."

Kylie walked past me and managed to jab me in the ribs with her bony elbow. I didn't miss the small grin on her lips. If I was wanting to keep my distance from her, I was doing a terrible job of it. I came over here to say goodbye to the cousins, not to flirt with Kylie.

Kylie hugged Mack. "I'm sorry I got mad at you for using my toothbrush. Just don't do it again."

She made her rounds, hugging each one. Then, they all took turns hugging me, too.

We traded phone numbers, and they all promised—or threatened—to get me to their family reunion one way or another. I wouldn't put kidnapping past them, so I wouldn't be surprised if I did end up at the family reunion somehow.

Jordan jumped into Page's car with her, and Jenny climbed into Mack's SUV. Jenny rolled the window down. "Hey, Kylie, I left you a few things in your purse. Just some self-defense things since we're not around."

She grinned and waved as she rolled the window back up. She probably left a cannon in Kylie's purse.

Kylie's eyes were misty as she watched them leave. I reached over and squeezed her shoulder—like a friend, of course, not a boyfriend who wanted to pull her in for a long hug.

"Sorry." She rubbed her cheeks. "I know it's silly, but I always hate to see my family go."

Forget being a friend. I was about to clear up the Brooke mess, anyway.

I tugged her toward me and wrapped my arms around her small frame. "Nothing silly about it. That means you love your family."

She laughed softly. "You'd think I'd be relieved that my house is still standing."

"Maybe those are relieved tears."

193

She laughed again before she stepped back out of my arms. "Thanks, Hagen. I guess that's the problem with growing up. Everyone goes their separate ways, and you can't keep everyone in a neat little box anymore."

"I know. It was tough for me and my brothers when we all got old enough to start doing different things. But no matter what we did, we would still be there for each other in a heartbeat. Your cousins are the same way. Look at the way they showed up here so soon when you needed them. You've got people in your life who care about you so much. That's because you would do the same thing for them."

She studied me for a minute. "You know, Hagen, for someone who wanted to not get involved in my life anymore, you seem a little interested."

I glared at her. She had me there. I wanted the best for her, but I couldn't seem to make myself stay away.

I couldn't even formulate a decent response, so I simply walked away.

Chapter Twenty-Five

KYLIE

S usan sent me home after half a day. I almost
bawled. She told me I wasn't focused and that I
should use some of my sick days that I never, ever used. I
couldn't believe I was so distracted at work. This was a job
I wanted to take seriously and make a career out of.

I'd told Susan what was on my mind, and she told me
to be patient with Hagen if I liked him that much—maybe
he would come around. Then, she sent me home anyway.

Susan was right to do so. All I could think of was
Hagen and how we had had such a great time together. I
wasn't getting any work done because I couldn't stop
thinking about how he had actually opened up—to me, of
all people—about his demanding ex-girlfriend. I wallowed
between raging anger and heart-brokenness.

I trudged up my walkway, not sure what to do with
myself. My house was clean, and Hagen had made me
promise not to start on the pergola without him. Not that
I'd even know where to begin if I did.

There was a small package sitting on my porch. I
turned around and went back down the sidewalk to check

my mail before I went into the house. Maybe I'd spend the rest of the day in athletic shorts, freezing in front of an air-conditioning vent. Maybe I'd find a new show to get addicted to and distract me from thinking about Hagen.

A sleek Jaguar pulled up outside of Hagen's house. A middle-aged woman stepped from the passenger side.

Hagen's mother. She had been there just a couple days ago. The day all my cousins left. I recognized her from the family pictures Hagen had in his house.

The driver's door opened, and I pretended to be preoccupied with opening my mailbox—until Brooke stepped out.

There was no way I could have pretended like I wasn't watching. I turned around and gave them a little wave. Brooke glanced at Hagen's mother—who shall remain nameless because I couldn't recall her name. Actually, I didn't think Hagen had ever told me.

Brooke said something I couldn't hear, then she started walking my way. I wondered if my panic was obvious on my face, because she had a small, albeit evil, smile on her perfect face.

"So, I get to see the little neighbor again."

I had to glance up at her. She must get tired of having her head in the clouds.

Brooke scowled.

Whoops. I must have said that out loud.

Then, she got down to her nasty business in a quiet voice. "Whatever hold you think you have on Hagen, it means nothing. You and him are nothing. He will end up with me one way or another."

I rested an elbow on my mailbox and studied the envelopes to try and stop my shaking hands. I hated confrontation. I was fairly certain confrontation hated me, too. But here I was, minding my own business, and Brooke decided to throw down the gauntlet.

"You haven't bagged him," she said.

What century had she stepped out of?

"Well, he didn't fit in my garbage can, so I don't think he'd fit in a bag," I muttered.

She took a step forward. "You're holding him back. By encouraging him to keep working at his silly little job, you're destroying his future. Yes, he told his mother how happy he is with his tiny projects. I know that's your doing. He could take over Glacier Bank someday, with me at his side. He has so much potential, but he's wasting away in suburbia."

I pointed at her with my handful of envelopes. "You have no idea the kind of man you dated. Have you even seen the stuff he builds? He's incredibly talented. He doesn't need a bunch of money to be amazing. He already is. And if you can't see that, then you don't deserve him either."

"He is throwing his life away as an electrician! He was born to be more, and I intend to be at his side as he rises to the top. You and his dreams will not stand in my way."

"So, remind me again, what is it you love about him? Is it the man or the money? Because he seems happy with his choice in careers. Not to mention, his woodworking business is taking off. Why can't you accept him as he is?"

Brooke folded her arms across her chest. "He doesn't know what's good for him. But trust me, I'll make him see. I've got his mother on my side. She wants to see us back together. She wants to see Hagen and me together again. And let me promise you, it will happen."

I noticed some movement behind Brooke, so I pretended to study my light-pink nails. "Have you told her that you refuse to have children? Even though Hagen wants a family? I guess I just don't understand how two such very different people could make a life together."

She took a step forward, and her cloud of perfume wafted over me. "We will make a life together because it's what I want. He'll get over his obsession with having a family when he's busy running Glacier Bank. There's nothing wrong with me refusing to become a mother!"

"You're right, dear," Hagen's mother said from where she stood behind Brooke. "What's wrong is the fact that you've lied to me, and you've lied about Hagen to me."

I bit my lip to keep from smiling. While Brooke had assumed Hagen's mother had gone into the house, I could see that she still stood by the car. She eventually made her way over right around the time Brooke started trashing Hagen's career choice.

I took a special delight in watching the color drain from Brooke's face. It only lasted a moment before Brooke pasted on a small, sweet smile and turned to the woman. "Lara, I'm sure you misunderstood what we were talking about. Kylie and I have a mutual friend—"

Lara held up a hand to stop her. "I think the only mutual friend you have is Hagen, and she was the one supporting him just now instead of tearing him down. Everything Hagen said makes sense now. He tried to spare you by not telling me the truth about you. It would be best if you go now."

Brooke tried one more time. "Lara, why don't I drive you home, and we'll talk about this?"

Lara shook her head. "I think I'm beginning to see the irreconcilable differences Hagen was talking about. Good-bye, Brooke."

Brooke looked between Lara and me a few times then walked to her car and drove off.

All I wanted to do was run straight into my house, lock

the door, and pretend like this little confrontation never happened, but Lara was standing there, looking at me expectantly.

"Hagen's probably still at work, but I have a spare key to his house I can get for you." I considered offering to let her hang out with me, but that sounded like hours of uncomfortable conversation, and I had come home with one plan in mind: to wallow.

Lara sighed. "That would be wonderful. My son and I have a long overdue conversation coming up."

I shut the mailbox and gave her a smile that didn't feel very bright. "Come on, I'll get the key for you."

I finished unlocking my house and turned off the alarm. Lara followed me inside and shut the door behind her. "What a lovely home."

I glanced around. My house was nearly exactly the same as Hagen's, but I had put in the effort to decorate it, whereas Hagen's walls and furniture had been bare until I added a few homey touches. "I enjoy decorating. Pinterest is a black hole for me."

Lara smiled and set her purse down on the entry table before walking into the living room.

She stopped next to my knitting basket. "Are you a crocheter?"

I rummaged through my giant purse, looking for Hagen's spare key. "Definitely not. A friend of mine, Hyacinth Perdue, is going to teach me how to knit. It won't be pretty."

"Hyacinth Perdue? She owns the craft shop downtown, doesn't she?"

I looked at her, surprised. "Why yes, she does! Do you know her?"

Lara nodded. "She plays bridge with my mother every week. She's a kind woman."

A door slammed, and we both looked out the big window to see Hagen stepping from his truck in the driveway. "Oh, he's home early. I hope everything's okay."

Lara gave me a strange look, and I pressed my lips together.

"Thank you for helping me."

I wasn't sure if she meant helping her with the spare key, bringing her inside in the cool air conditioning, or exposing the truth about Brooke, so I simply smiled and nodded and used my best client voice. "You have a great day now."

She looked me over once more before she grabbed her purse off the table and headed outside.

Chapter Twenty-Six

HAGEN

*W*e finished up early with our latest job. We weren't due to start our next house until next Monday, which meant I had an extra long weekend.

When I looked over at Kylie's house, I saw the strangest sight. Stranger than Kylie tackling Jordan in the yard. Stranger than Jenny on the roof with a paintball gun. Stranger than Kylie's reindeer pajamas.

It was my mother, stepping out of Kylie's house. I was pretty sure my jaw dropped to the ground. Mom crossed the street and patted my arm as she passed me. "We need to talk."

I turned and followed her into the garage, closed the big door, and opened the door into the house. "Come on in; I'll get you something to drink."

"I hope it's strong."

That didn't exactly make me want to find out what had happened over at Kylie's house. Turned out, the only strong drink I had in the house was a sweet wine that Kylie had left behind. It was a little flat, but I poured Mom a glass anyway. She didn't seem to mind when she took the first sip. I grabbed myself a water from the fridge.

"Why didn't you tell me?" Mom's voice had an edge to it, just like it did when I was little and my brothers and I had gotten into big trouble.

"I'm not sure what we're talking about."

"Brooke. The family business. Why you really broke up with her?"

I felt the blood drain from my face. "What did Kylie say?"

I had wanted the chance to tell Mom the truth. I knew she would be hurt since she considered Brooke a friend.

Mom shook her head and took a big drink of her wine.

"It was Brooke. She drove me here."

That explained why I didn't see my mom's car outside.

"Why was Brooke here?"

Mom waved her hand through the air. "Because I didn't understand. Why didn't you tell me?"

I sat down on Kylie's favorite barstool and rubbed a thumb between my eyebrows. "Mom, you're going to have to back up and explain everything from the beginning."

She began pacing back and forth in front of the kitchen sink. "I thought you wanted to be in the family business. She kept telling me you didn't feel welcome. She told me that you didn't want to pressure your father by asking to be a part."

I'd wondered why my mom had hounded me so much to be a part of Glacier Bank. My parents were the ones who had fostered my love of building things. Dad was the one who got me my first circuit board kit when I was eleven. It hadn't made sense that they would encourage me in my work then, all of a sudden, want me to switch to finance.

"Why don't we go sit down?" I suggested. I grabbed

another water bottle from the fridge before I sat in my favorite spot on the couch.

"I only wanted you to be happy. I know you've wanted a family. I thought Brooke would be perfect for you since you wanted the same things." She studied her pink nails.

"Mom, what did Kylie say to you?"

Mom shook her head. "It wasn't her; I already told you. It was what Brooke said and the way that girl jumped in to defend you. No wonder you seemed infatuated with her last time I was here."

I ducked my head to hide my grin. The idea of Kylie standing up for me made my chest feel like it was going to explode. She cared, even though I kept trying to shut her out.

"Brooke has lied about everything, hasn't she?"

"What made you realize?"

"When she was busy tearing you apart to the neighbor girl. That girl came back swinging and told Brooke exactly what she thought."

"She punched Brooke?"

"No, of course not. That was metaphorical, of course."

I chuckled, because what my mother hadn't realized yet was that Kylie might very well smack someone who verbally attacked someone she loved.

Mom continued. "With neighbors like that, you don't have anything to worry about. Unless you're more than neighbors."

She looked at me pointedly. Trust my mother to be upset about Brooke's betrayal and instantly start trying to matchmake me with Kylie.

She really wanted more grandbabies.

"Why didn't you tell me what Brooke was really like?"

"You seemed to enjoy spending time with her. I didn't want to ruin the friendship you had with her."

She reached over and patted my leg. "I won't say another word about Brooke. And I won't pester you to join the family business. Just know that we will always keep that open to you."

I leaned over and kissed her slightly wrinkled cheek. "Thanks, Mom. I'm sorry I didn't say anything sooner. I'm glad you know the truth now. It felt like Brooke was managing to drive a wedge between us."

"I agree. Now it makes sense why. Social climber. What a silly girl."

I couldn't help but agree with Mom's summary of Brooke's ambitions. There was so much more to life than money and social position. I was grateful those were lessons that my parents had bothered to teach me as I grew up.

Chapter Twenty-Seven

KYLIE

I swiped a layer of matte rose on my lips before I grabbed my purse and headed out the door. It was Friday, but I had an 8:30 meeting with Jason at the office. We were going to go over a few more concepts for his campaign, including a radio ad we would run on local stations. I was hoping he would agree to be the voice for it. It was his gym, after all.

I started my car and turned the air conditioner on full blast. It was going to be a scorcher again today.

I felt clammy as I stepped from the car. I wanted to let it cool down before I drove anywhere.

Hagen's truck sat in his driveway, and every time I looked at it, my heart sped up. It was my own Pavlov response to knowing Hagen was home. Hagen may have said that he wanted to move on, but his words didn't match his actions. He kept coming up with ridiculous excuses to come over and see me. Not to mention, I'd found a pile of lumber in my backyard. I could have only assumed it was the beginnings of a pergola. *My pergola*. His head and his heart weren't lined up quite right, but I didn't mind waiting. It would be worth it. He was worth it. Even if he didn't realize it.

He liked me. I knew it. That was why I was willing to wait for him to have the self-confidence to see how great he was. Self-discovery wasn't something you could rush.

Of course, I'd make sure he didn't forget me in the meantime.

I crossed the street and glanced around for Hagen. He hadn't left yet. I stepped onto the running board of the pickup and slipped a couple of rubber spiders through the crack. I noticed the look of disgust on his face when he found a spider in my kitchen sink the other day. I hoped he screamed like a little girl. Unfortunately, I didn't have time to hang around and find out. I needed to get to the office for that meeting with Jason.

I pulled into the small parking lot behind the office and shut off my car. I pulled my keys from the ignition, checked my lipstick one more time, then dropped my keys in my giant purse before I climbed out and locked the car.

When I turned around, I came face to face with Lyle. "Lyle! You scared me. What are you doing here today?"

He swallowed a couple times before he spoke. "I've been waiting for you."

"Oh, I didn't know you were coming in today since it's Friday and all. You must have gotten here early. It's not even eight-thirty yet."

"We need to talk." He coughed.

"I have a meeting this morning, but if you have time early Monday—"

He pulled his hand from behind his back and pointed a pistol at me. "Now, Kylie. I'm so sorry it had to come to this. I tried to be nice. I tried to be patient, but you wouldn't listen."

He was legitimately pointing a gun at my chest. I didn't

think this happened in real life. The mild-mannered office assistants were supposed to be Superman—not a super-villain. Why would he be pointing a gun at me? Sweat ran down my back, making my blouse cling to me even tighter. My grip on my purse was turning slippery.

"Get in my car and I won't have to hurt you." He sounded as though he were on the verge of tears. "I don't want to hurt you, but I can't watch you be with someone else."

I took a few wobbly steps toward his car when he pressed the gun into my side. He hit the key fob, unlocking it for me to climb in. He slammed the door after me and managed to keep the gun trained on me while he walked around and climbed into the driver's seat.

I'd always thought if I had ever gotten kidnapped, my adrenaline rush would kick in and I would have the strength of Superman. I figured I would fight tooth and nail and that my attacker would regret laying eyes on me.

Yes, I had spent considerable amounts of my life wondering "what if" this worst-case scenario happened to me.

Now I knew. And it wasn't pretty. Instead of over-whelming him with my superior strength, I had quietly gotten into his car and buckled my seat belt. It was like my body was on autopilot, conducting itself with self-preserva-tion in mind.

No fits of rage. No overpowering my kidnapper.

He kept the gun trained on me as he started the car and backed out of the parking lot. He made me hand over my phone and set my purse on the ground. I readily complied when he gestured with the gun.

I did switch the radio channel to something classical. It was my one act of defiance, and I hoped the soothing tones would calm him down. He didn't seem to even notice. He kept furtively glancing in his rearview mirror, and I kept glancing at my phone that rested in his lap.

If I could steal it back, I could call for help.

Except that wasn't going to happen.

"Here," Lyle said as he handed me my phone.

Wow. I underestimated the power of positive thinking.

"Nothing funny. No calls, no texts other than what I tell you."

"What do you want me to do?"

"Text Hagen and break up with him. There's going to be nothing between us anymore."

"But we're—"

"I don't want to hear a single word about your boyfriend!" Lyle screamed. His mouth was open so wide I could count his teeth. He must have had his wisdom teeth pulled.

My fingers shook as I unlocked my phone screen. "What do you want me to tell him?"

"Tell him you're done, that you're not going to date him anymore."

"How did you know we were dating?"

"I saw you!" he screamed again. He had a loud set of lungs for someone so thin. "I saw you, and I won't allow anyone to stand in our way. Text him now."

My mind raced as I hurried to text Hagen like he asked.

Lyle was the one responsible for all the notes. He was my stalker. And right now, I had one chance to get myself out of this mess and it involved Hagen. I only hoped this wouldn't get either of us killed.

Chapter Twenty-Eight

HAGEN

*R*ick took a giant bite of his burrito. We sat in a police cruiser close to downtown. He had called me early that morning and told me he had something important to tell me then asked me to bring lunch.

As I ate my street tacos, I felt like a giant weight had been lifted off my chest. Whatever Rick had to tell me couldn't have taken away that feeling. My mother knew the truth about Brooke. My dad had texted me this morning to see if I had time to look at an electrical problem in his office. It was his way of giving me a pat on the back.

The nagging hold that Brooke had on my life was gone. My family knew the truth and wouldn't support her any longer. She wouldn't be around to cause any more problems for me and definitely wouldn't be able to verbally attack Kylie. Having the truth out meant I was free to go to family dinners on Sundays. And most importantly, it meant I was free to date Kylie. Nothing stood in the way now.

"Hagen, I didn't want to have to tell you this," Rick said slowly.

"What?"

"The guy we arrested for the break-ins wasn't the man who sent the notes to Kylie."

"What do you mean?"

"I mean, he told us that he saw another man taking pictures of her and following her the same time he was. He passed the polygraph."

"Those things aren't one hundred percent."

"Yes, you're right, but he also told us he wasn't the one who broke into Kylie's house."

I slammed my fist against the dashboard. "How is that possible?"

"When he started casing out her house, he figured she was too young and healthy to have any prescription drugs in her place, and she always took her laptop with her. Figured it'd be a waste of time because she didn't leave anything behind with any resale value. Said the TV was the size of my microwave."

"Well, he was right about the TV size, but maybe he's lying to have a lighter sentence."

"He's not. He had an alibi for that day, and it checks out. Someone else broke into Kylie's house. This guy fessed up to all the other break-ins because it would lessen his sentence."

"Have you called Kylie yet?"

"No." He frowned. "I was hoping you could help me with that. I told her she could relax since we caught the guy, when really that couldn't be further from the truth."

"What do you mean?"

Rick looked me in the eye. "She suspected she being stalked. I'm sure she told you."

"Yes, I saw the pictures."

"Well, our perp didn't take those. Like I said, he told us about noticing another guy hanging around."

I sat back in the seat and ran a hand over my face.

She'd been alone in her house for a couple days. I'd assumed the worst thing that could have happened to her was she could have dated me. Right now, I wished I hadn't been so stubborn and warped with my thinking. Thank goodness nothing had happened. I'd pick her up from the office, and she would stay with me again.

I pulled my phone out of my pocket to give her a call. There was already a text message from her. She'd sent it a couple hours ago. I hadn't checked it since I'd left for work earlier that morning.

Kylie:
  Hagen,
  Even though you thought we'd be a couple, we won't.
  Lyle & I are together.
  Please.
  Move on for me.
  Exactly how you should.

"Rick, look at this." I passed him my phone.

"Hmm, looks like she doesn't want anything to do with you."

"She put a fake spider in my truck this morning."

"She's vindictive?"

"Why would she text me? I told her we wouldn't work out."

"Call and make sure everything's alright," Rick suggested.

I had already dialed her number. It rang three times then went straight to voicemail. I left her a quick message urging her to call me back.

I looked at the message again. "Who the heck is Lyle?"

Rick crunched a chip loudly. "Maybe an old boyfriend. They're usually the ones who turn into stalkers. But this just sounds like she's tired of your crap."

"No, she told me about her old boyfriends. Lyle wasn't one of them. Something's wrong; I can feel it. If only I could remember who Lyle was. Look at this. Look at the way she capitalized the message."

Rick glanced over my shoulder. "Is she at work today?"

"She was supposed to be. I'll call the office." I quickly looked up the number for SV Marketing. I dialed and waited; someone finally answered. "Hello, I'm trying to reach Kylie Boone. Is she in the office right now?"

"No, I'm sorry. She didn't come in today."

"I thought she had a meeting today."

There was a pause and rustling on the other end of the line. "Who is this?"

"My name is Hagen Raglund. I'm her neighbor."

"Ah, the neighbor. Well, I'm Susan VandenMeyer, and I'm glad you called, because I was beginning to get a little worried for her. She's never missed a meeting. Lyle was here too, but——"

"What was that name you said?"

That had to be the answer. "You mean Lyle?"

"Yes. Where does he live?"

"Well, I certainly can't be giving out my employees' addresses to strangers."

Rick reached over and put my phone on speakerphone. "Hello, ma'am, this is detective Rick Wiggins, and I'm afraid we have a little bit of a situation. I would appreciate all the help you could give."

We quickly explained what had been going on with Kylie getting stalked and her house being broken into. Susan searched through the files and told us Lyle's address without hesitation. Her only request was that we made sure Kylie made it back to her whole and healthy.

"Let's go check on this Lyle," I told Rick as I buckled my seatbelt.

"Hold up there, Ranger Bill. We can't just go barging into his house because we suspect something."

"But it has to be him."

"I agree with you, but the court of law wouldn't look favorably on an officer barging into a house based only on a hunch."

I cleared my throat. "You can't. You're right. Thank goodness I'm here."

Chapter Twenty-Nine

KYLIE

Someone knocked on the door. Lyle jumped. I tried not to scream.

He pulled the gun out of the back of his pants and stared at the door like there was a monster behind it. I sincerely hoped it wasn't Hagen. I'd been kicking myself for the last couple hours for texting him in code. I'd wanted to be saved. I hadn't wanted to make Hagen walk into a bullet.

Lyle flipped the deadbolt.

I stood up quietly and bent down so I could step over my zip-tied hands. If something was about to happen, I didn't want to be stuck with my hands behind my back.

When we had pulled up to his dingy little duplex, he'd carried my purse and phone in one hand and kept a gun trained on me with the other. He'd ushered me inside the stuffy home and then put zip ties around my wrists as a "precaution."

I glanced around the room for something to use as a weapon, but unless I learned how to kill someone with a pen—Jason Bourne style—then I was out of luck.

Lyle opened the door a few inches, but it was enough that I could see who stood on the other side.

"You!" he yelled.

Before I had a chance to warn Hagen, Lyle swung the door open and fired three shots.

I screamed, imagining Hagen's body riddled with bullets. Lyle stepped back behind the door and yelled, "Get inside!"

Hagen stepped through the door, and I sobbed with relief. "He shot you."

Lyle slammed and bolted the door. He swung around and pointed his gun at Hagen. "Sit down."

Hagen started to sit next to me, but Lyle stopped him.

"No, not there. You sit over there." He motioned across the room, and I scanned Hagen for any signs of a bullet wound. There wasn't any visible blood, and he was walking as easily as usual.

He gave me a wink before he crossed to the other side and sat on a faded black futon. I wondered who Lyle had been shooting at since I didn't see any wounds on Hagen.

"Lyle, this isn't something you want to do. You'd better just let us go and we can forget this whole thing."

Lyle kept the gun pointed in Hagen's direction as he ran a hand through his hair. "Shut up."

"Man, it's hot in here. Did your air conditioner quit?" Hagen pointed at Lyle's chest that was soaked with sweat.

"None of your business."

"You know, I'm pretty handy with fixing stuff. I could take a look at it and get it working again."

Lyle grabbed the gun with two hands and shook it in Hagen's direction. "I said, shut up!"

I tried to work my hands loose from the zip ties. With sweaty wrists, it was getting easier to slip the zip ties farther up my hands. Not that I knew what I was going to do with free hands, but I didn't want Hagen to be facing a psychotic gunman alone.

I couldn't believe how I'd missed all the signs that pointed to Lyle. His obsession with being near me at work. His endless questions about my personal life. His observance.

He'd spent the last hour detailing his obsession with me. He even showed me albums on his laptop of all the pictures he'd taken of me over the past couple months. He talked about his plans for our future and our life together. I'd had an overwhelming urge to vomit. Something was not right in his mind.

"Be quiet and let me think." Lyle began pacing back and forth, keeping a constant eye on Hagen and ignoring me. Too bad that superhero strength was still evading me. When I got back to the gym, I was going to take a weights class from Jason.

Ten minutes later, Lyle was sitting on the couch next to me, tapping the gun against his leg. I still didn't know what he'd been shooting at out the door, and I didn't want to ask. I was afraid it might set him off again.

Lyle stood up and peeked out the curtains. He cursed quietly. "This isn't what I wanted to happen." He waved the gun at Hagen. "Stand up."

"Thank goodness; my leg was starting to fall asleep. How do you sit on that thing? It's got to be the most uncomfortable couch in the world."

Hagen's laid-back attitude was nearly making me cry. Having him here with me in this situation was giving me enough strength to not have a complete breakdown.

Lyle stood up straight. "My mom gave it to me."

"I know of a great little furniture shop—"

"Shut up!" Lyle screamed. His forehead was turning

an unnatural shade of red. "You're making this so much easier on me. Kneel down."

"I'm not going to be able to fix that air conditioning unit if I'm kneeling down." Hagen shrugged one shoulder as if it were his one goal in life to fix that AC unit.

"Kylie, grab your purse. We're leaving," Lyle said to me with a twisted smile. I thought he had meant for it to be reassuring, but all I saw was an unhinged man waving a gun at the man I loved.

I glanced around for anything I could have used to distract Lyle long enough for Hagen to get away, but I doubted Hagen was the type to leave me behind.

I walked to my purse sitting on the small shelf. He hadn't let me touch it since he forced me into his car. I thought he was afraid I carried a flare signal in there. When I grasped the handle of my giant bag, I remembered what I did have in there. It wasn't a flare signal, but Jenny really had left me some things to defend myself: bear spray, a collapsible baton, and brass knuckles.

God bless Jenny and her sense of overkill.

The bear spray would have been a bad idea in a small room. We would have all suffered the consequences. Punching people wasn't exactly my forte—that was more of a Jenny move.

But if I could open the baton, I could at least knock the gun out of his hand.

"Get on your knees now!" Lyle yelled at Hagen as he peeked through the curtain again.

Hagen slowly complied, and Lyle walked over to stand between me and Hagen. I watched in horror as he leveled his gun at the back of Hagen's head.

He was going to kill him, execution style.

This was not how I had envisioned my Friday going when I climbed out of bed this morning. I had wanted to initiate "Operation Convince Hagen We're Meant to Be," not "Operation Try to Keep Hagen Alive."

"You really don't want to do this, man," Hagen said.

I fumbled around in my purse until I found the baton. Lyle didn't even turn around. The zip ties cut into my wrists as I tried to extend it. I shook it.

Lyle looked back and forth between Hagen's head and the window that he couldn't see out of.

I found a button on the end of the baton and pushed it. It extended with a soft sigh. Thank goodness it wasn't armed with a blaring siren or a built-in whistle.

"I didn't want to do this," Lyle told Hagen in a strained voice.

I brought the baton above my head and swung it down on him right where his shoulder met his neck. His reflex made his arm fold up, bringing the gun up in the air, away from Hagen's head.

Lyle let out a scream that would have put Jordan to shame.

Pulling back, I took a swing at the back of his legs. Hagen jumped out of the way and grabbed the gun from Lyle's hands as he toppled over.

"Good grief, woman. You've got a heck of a swing."

Hagen wrapped an arm around my shoulders and pulled me against his left side. He kept the pistol trained on Lyle, who lay on the ground, cradling his shoulder.

Hagen backed us up closer to the window and opened the curtains with his gun hand. I didn't think Lyle would attempt to take on Hagen without a weapon, but I was glad when Hagen pointed the weapon back in Lyle's direction.

I had always been a little intimidated by guns. In fact, after Lyle had pulled that one on me in the parking lot, I'd been downright terrified. But with Hagen holding the pistol, I felt safe. I forgot all about why I was terrified of guns. As a matter of fact, I was pretty glad we had that gun right then.

Hagen slid the window open and yelled outside. "Hey, Rick, I think it's okay to come in now!"

The front door slammed inward, and three police officers I didn't recognize stormed into the living room with their guns drawn. One of them cuffed Lyle and pulled him up to stand while reading him his rights.

Rick followed them inside, along with the older detective, Jim, who helped on the night Lyle broke into my house.

Rick stepped over and held out a bag for Hagen to place the pistol in.

Hagen reluctantly removed his arm from my shoulder, and I had to pry my fingers loose from where I hung on to his t-shirt.

Jim pulled out a knife and cut the zip tie from my wrists.

The second my wrists were free, Hagen spun me around, pulled me into his arms, and kissed me square on the mouth, his strong hands on my back and shoulders, lending me his strength. His kiss reminded me that I had something to look forward to in the midst of this mess.

Someone cleared their throat.

Hagen pulled back just enough to rest his forehead on mine. He brushed his hand along the side of my head, gently pushing my hair behind my ear.

"I thought I was going to lose you," he whispered.

Rick came up behind Hagen and placed a hand on his shoulder. "Don't worry, there will be time for that later. Right now, I have a report to file."

Hagen turned to glare at him. "You have the worst timing."

Rick grinned. "I know. Why don't we go outside while you tell us what happened? It's a little too hot in here."

With a nod, I followed him out the door with Hagen right behind me, his hand resting on my lower back. I couldn't get out of that duplex fast enough.

The questions that followed were a little bit too much of deja vu from the last time I talked to Jim and Rick. I told them everything that happened, beginning with me pulling into work, to sitting in Lyle's house when Hagen knocked.

I told him how Lyle had admitted to following me and breaking into my house because he was jealous. It was embarrassing to share that part. Lyle told me that when he saw my cactus on the counter, he'd gotten angry at my deception. He wanted me to feel hurt the same way I had hurt him.

Hagen reassured me about fifty times that none of this was my fault. I hated to remind him that it was my text that brought him to Lyle's and almost got him killed.

When the police finally finished with their questioning, Rick dropped us off at Hagen's truck downtown. Hagen drove us back home. He backed into my driveway and walked around to open my door for me.

I felt like my mind was still stuck on a merry-go-round.

Lyle had stalked me.

Lyle kidnapped me.

Lyle tried to kill Hagen.

The same thoughts played on a circular loop in my head like a flashing billboard.

Hagen unlocked my door with his key and shut the alarm off before he led me into the kitchen. He rummaged through my junk drawers and pulled out the first aid kit. It almost felt like the last time he had done this, right after I biffed it with the snake—the fake snake.

Except, this time, I knew Hagen. I knew the type of man he was.

Hagen shook his head as he held my wrists under the faucet and gently cleaned off the dried blood. "When I realized what had happened, I almost lost my mind."

I nodded. I was afraid if I opened my mouth, I would start balling. My wrists were chafed from where the zip ties had dug into my skin. Future note to self: zip ties are stronger than my skin, and no amount of pulling or twisting will change that fact.

Hagen continued. "When he was waving his gun around, I was so afraid you were going to get hurt."

I hiccupped, and the tears started to fall. Hagen shut off the water and wrapped my wrists with a soft kitchen towel before he ushered me into the living room. He sat down on the couch and gently pulled me onto his lap. He wrapped his strong arms around me and rested his chin on my head.

I stopped fighting the tears. Crying allowed me to release the terror, relief, and shock. I hadn't thought it was possible to experience all of those emotions at the same time. Hagen rubbed his hand in small circles on my back.

I didn't know how long we sat like that, but I knew that I went through all stages of ugly crying before I grabbed some tissues off the coffee table and tried to clean up my face. My voice shook when I spoke. "I was so scared that he was going to shoot you."

Hagen snorted. "You do realize that you were the one who got kidnapped and held hostage today? Yet, your first worry was that I might be killed." He pressed a kiss against my temple and tucked me close to his side.

"When he made you kneel down, it was like I saw you lying there dead already. I've never been so scared in my life."

"Well, you saved my life. You know what that means, don't you?"

I shook my head, and he smiled.

"In some cultures, when you save someone's life, that person becomes indebted to you for the rest of their life. Sometimes, they even become their servant. So, I guess you're looking at your new man slave."

I laughed, and then Hagen laughed with me, and then we were both laughing hysterically. "Imagine all of the honey-do chores I would give you. I would happily never touch a tool again."

He pressed his lips together. "I hope you know I'm serious. When I thought about losing you, I couldn't handle it. I don't ever want to lose you. I want to try and be everything you deserve."

"You're an idiot."

He jerked back like I'd slapped him.

"I love you exactly how you are. I don't want you to change."

His face relaxed into a smile. "You mean that, don't you?"

"Yes. I think you're amazing right now, and I love getting to be around you."

"You love me."

My cheeks warmed. Had I let that slip out? I meant to make him feel good about himself, not scare him away with my feelings."

"I think I like that."

I ran a hand over my face and groaned. "I didn't mean to make things weird."

He raised an eyebrow as he looked down at me. "You made things weird when you threatened to shove me in your trashcan. I think telling me that you love me is the least of your worries."

I studied the ceiling and wondered what it would look like if I painted it navy.

"Why did you change the lock on my garbage can?" I had to ask. Really, if he hadn't done that, we never would have stepped into a full-on prank war and fallen for each other.

He traced his fingers up and down my arm. "There was this look in your eye. The day you stood on your porch and laughed about locking me out of your garbage can. You looked so full of life, so happy about doing something like that. I knew I had to get to know you more. I had hoped you would stand up to me. I liked seeing that spark in your eye. I think it helped me rediscover the happiness in life that I'd been missing out on this last year."

I leaned closer to him, resting my head on his shoulder.

"You know I love you too, Kylie. That's why I wanted to stay away. I'm never going to be different than who I am. I wanted the best for you. I didn't want Brooke or my own insecurities to come between us. I needed that distance to clear up everything with Brooke. I needed her completely out of our lives so she couldn't hurt you. I needed my family to know the truth so that I could move forward with what I felt for you."

I looked at him. "Don't you realize you are the best for me? I love you. You. Not some stupid job or money. All that stuff isn't important. I love the guy who shuts off my water and leaves fake snakes in my shower—okay, maybe not that one. I love the guy who just marched into a house with an armed madman to save me. Good grief, I'd be crazy not to love someone who's willing to do that."

He grinned and leaned down to kiss my head and whispered, "I thought I was going to pee my pants."

"That's the most romantic thing you've ever told me."

He smiled. "I love you, Kylie. You didn't give up on

me, even when I tried to push you away. I even forgive you for shooting me with the paintball gun."

"That's pretty big of you."

"I know. I'm a class act like that."

Without warning, he leaned down and pressed is mouth against mine. Grasping the sides of my face, he tilted his head to the side so he could kiss me deeper. One hand moved around to my lower back. My breath caught as he pulled me tight against his chest. He didn't act like he was going to stop anytime soon.

I ran both my hands through his messed-up hair, wanting him closer. Wanting to know that he was mine. Wanting to know I could tease, and tug, and love him. Wanting to show him exactly how I felt with our kiss.

I conveyed all these things with action, and he responded in the same language.

EPILOGUE

Hagen

"*W*hat's this small square box?" Jenny yelled.

I was going to kill her. I set down my hamburger and took a drink of Coke while I contemplated the best way to kill someone when there were a hundred witnesses.

Kylie's family surrounded me. Despite my best efforts, I'd been forced into the family reunion. I never knew there were so many people that could be related. Mimi, the grandma I'd heard so much about, sat to my left. Page sat to my right, and Kylie was nowhere to be found. Maybe I could cut Jenny off before she showed the entire country-side the engagement ring I'd had specially made for Kylie.

"Excuse me, Mimi." The black-haired woman smiled at me as I climbed out of the fifteen-foot picnic table that I had built specifically for the reunion. I'd made four in total, and we planned on leaving them at Mimi's. Her place was where all the reunions and any major holiday happened. They needed more seating since having a hundred guests was considered a small crowd.

"Hey, Hagen!" Jenny yelled as I weaved past a group of small children. "There's something in here, what is it?"

Just as Jenny was about to open the box, I snatched it out of her hand and put it in my pocket. "How'd you get that? I left it locked in my truck."

Jenny grinned and shrugged. "Oh look, there's Kylie. Why don't you ask her if the box is hers?"

I gritted my teeth. "Someday, I'll get even with you for this."

She just smiled as I turned around to face Kylie, the suspiciously shaped ring box still in my pocket. The family that sat closest to us grew silent.

"Hagen, what's going on?" Kylie asked as she looked between Jenny, me, and all the eyes on us. Then her gaze landed on my jeans pocket. It didn't help that I had my hand in it as if I could hide the shape of the box.

"Do it," Jenny urged quietly. I wondered if she would ever move away from Louisiana. I'd help pack her bags.

I swiped my sweaty palms on my jeans, then pulled out the ring box, and climbed down on one knee in front of Kylie, who wore one of her favorite jumpsuit things. It was bright yellow—my favorite color on her. She never failed to look amazing.

Her shocked face started to crack into a smile as I flipped open the box.

"Kylie Boone, I'm not looking for a girlfriend."

Her eyes narrowed.

"But I am looking for a wife. There is no one else in the world that I can imagine spending the rest of my life with. I love you with all of my heart. I'm sorry I didn't get to give you a romantic proposal at sunset on the beach like I'd planned. But here, you're surrounded by the people you love, and who love you. Family who would do anything for you. I want to be that to you, too. Would you do me the honor of becoming my wife? Will you marry me?"

"Yes!" She leapt toward me. I barely had time to jump to my feet and catch her as she flew through the air.

And I knew, right then, what it felt like to hold the whole world in my arms.

THE END

I hope you enjoyed Kylie and Hagen's story! I love hearing what readers liked most about a story, so don't forget to leave a review and tell me!

If you'd like to know about future books, and sneak peeks, you can sign up for the Carina Taylor newsletter here!

ACKNOWLEDGMENTS

Thank you to everyone who helped with this book. My awesome critique partners who helped set the tone for the entire book. The beta readers that fine-tuned everything with me. Jenn, for being amazing and detailed.

Thank you to all of my ARC readers!

Thank you to my boys who have been my little cheerleaders and have told me they're going to write a book someday—I hope they do.

They say it takes a village to raise a child. The same could be said about writing a book. This wouldn't have been even half the story it is without all the help I had! I hope this book has made you smile or gulp your lemonade too fast. That would make me incredibly happy.

A LOVE LIKE THIS SERIES

WHAT'S NEXT?

Christmas Like This #2 in A Love Like This
I know exactly what I'd like to put in Trey's stocking: the biggest lump of coal I can carry.
Unfortunately, I won't get the chance, because our boss has delivered an ultimatum: plan the company Christmas party with Trey and learn to get along, or else.
After only one day of trying to plan the Christmas party, I'm ready to pick the "or else." Is it possible to learn to get along with the most aggravating, overprotective, handsome guy I've ever known?
We're about to find out if we can get our names off the naughty list or not.

Friends Like These #3 in A Love Like This

What do you get when you take over a failing golf course? A woman.

My grandfather left me his golf course so he could enjoy an early retirement. Unfortunately, it wasn't the only thing he left for me...

Page comes to my golf course—winning the hearts and minds of (most) my staff by permanently relocating the deadly mascot left by my grandfather.

This beautiful woman with a million terrible ideas and a wanderer's heart is determined to help me.
I don't need her help—but I can't seem to tell her no, even if I end up being the proud owner of a one-legged chicken.

Page Boone is going to drive me crazy—and I wouldn't have it any other way.

READ MORE FROM CARINA TAYLOR:

Love On Willow Loop *(A short romantic comedy)*
The Perfect Plan *(a small town romance)*

Mr. H.O.A. (A romantic comedy)
Bane Fox knows exactly what he wants in life: financial stability.

He does *not* want to be homeless.
He does *not* want to be the president of an HOA.

It's rather unfortunate he is both of those things.

Oh, and did I forget to mention he has a fake wife?
Yeah, that's me.

Miss Trailerhood (A romantic comedy)
She disappeared from our lives without a word. I never expected to run into her at a Quik Mart in between jobs. What's a guy to do when he finds his first crush? Follow her

home, of course, and remind her of all the things she's missing.

I didn't know that holding onto Riley would involve living in a trailer park. Or keeping it a secret from my sister—*her best friend.*

Riley is completely at home with lawn-mower racing, beer-guzzling exhibitionists. She doesn't think I can handle it. Well, I'm going to show Miss Trailerhood that I'm here to stay—no matter what trailer-park mayhem she puts me through.

Love is patient, love is kind, love means buying a single wide.

Made in United States
North Haven, CT
21 July 2022

21679281R00134